Kelly

Journey to Forever

Happy Journeys to You

Anne Edmondson Barbour

Anne Edmondson Barbour

Second in the Love Connections Series

Readers are encouraged to go to www.MissionPointPress.com to contact the author or to find information on how to buy this book in bulk at a discounted rate.

Published by Mission Point Press
2554 Chandler Rd.
Traverse City, MI 49696
(231) 421-9513
www.MissionPointPress.com

ISBN: 978-1-950659-95-1

Library of Congress Control Number: 2021900469

Printed in the United States of America

One

Jerilyn Tate was on a plane that had just taken off from the Kansas City airport. She thought, *This is much different than my first trip to Nebraska, when Maggie and I drove to visit Austen. This time I'm flying—alone—to her wedding. But in truth, it's mainly to see someone I hardly know. A man I've only met once, but who has come to mean so much to me.*

As they headed west, she recalled that first trip and meeting Josh Wilson. Hard to believe it was only a couple of months ago. Now, here she was on a plane going toward him. Was it a journey for love?

~

Austen Wiley surprised everyone, including her parents, when mostly on a whim, she applied for a job in Nebraska. The ad she responded to stated: "would consider a family." Hoping she would be able to spend more time with David, her four-year-old son, she quit her well-paying job, then drove toward her future. Her being hired was a last-minute occurrence, and it was only after she got there that she learned one of TrailWays' main functions in the summer was to provide experiences on the Oregon Trail.

Austen had shared only enough about the trip and her job with them to create curiosity in her group of church friends. Then after her mother visited and described the man who owned the place and was her daughter's boss, there were more questions—especially since Mrs. Morgan told them Austen and David were living in the owner's house with him. What did that mean anyway, and why?

All of Austen's friends in the group talked about visiting her to see for themselves. But only Jerilyn and Maggie West were able to do so, knowing that if they were to make a visit, it needed to be soon, as summer days were racing by. Jerilyn was a teacher and orientation would be in less than a month.

As they traveled across Nebraska, each made note of the countryside and the wide-open spaces. It would look different now than when Austen saw it in the spring. It was late summer, and crops were about ready to be harvested. Jerilyn thought her mother would have made special note of the wildflowers in the fields; she might even have known their names.

Thinking of the animals that would have populated the area at the time of the wagon trains, Jerilyn could see them in her mind: pronghorns, prairie dogs, even buffalo, which would have been plentiful then.

It was a different experience. Both Jerilyn and Maggie were accustomed to driving in the city with its constant traffic, not sharing a highway with semis. The only time they might have noticed the rural areas and farmland of Kansas would have been when they had reason to travel to another nearby town.

As the miles piled up behind them, Jerilyn's thoughts were on those hardy pioneers who had traveled to Oregon in wagon trains and would have traveled along this very same route. No highways then; the wagons made their own, which became ruts, still seen in a few areas even today, almost two hundred years later. She wondered if she would have been one of those settlers. How would she have felt about making such an extreme change in her life? Would she have been a single woman, maybe even a teacher hoping to meet someone who would be her future? Or would she already have a family, worried about her young children, but excited to be traveling to a place that offered new beginnings?

They reached TrailWays at five o'clock on a Tuesday afternoon after a long trip of hundreds of miles, and many hours. But it probably wasn't as tiring for them as it must have been for Austen. She was the only driver, plus David, her young son, was with her, and required more stops than two adult females needed. They had let Austen know when they would be there on that August day, so a cabin was reserved for them.

Austen was there to meet them, as were Kate and Bill Pearson, managers of the place. Soon after their arrival, the Pony Express Rider for the treks rode in carrying some letters to be mailed and was introduced to them as Josh Wilson. Kate took the opportunity to mention he was a teacher too and was also single. Did the woman have matchmaking in mind?

Neither Josh nor Jerilyn minded. He had a cute flirtatious grin for her, and she sent one back his way. She was only there for a few days, so there was no expectation that anything more than friendship would develop.

But the day Austen took Jerilyn and Maggie on a short trek, Josh had Pony Express mail to deliver, and asked Jerilyn to ride back to headquarters with him. Her arms around him on that ride was about as close as they came to anything that could be considered romantic, but somehow it felt like the beginning of something special.

There were no plans for the next day, but Austen suggested they drive into Plattsford to visit some of the businesses. When he heard that, Mark Thomas, owner of TrailWays and Austen's boss, asked if he could go too. Glancing at Austen, Jerilyn and Maggie could see she hadn't expected that. But they welcomed the opportunity to see the couple together, thinking of the report Austen's mother had made.

On their way to the nearby town, Mark told them Josh would meet them at the grocery store. After he arrived, they walked around the town, visiting some of the other businesses before ending up back at the grocery store. From there, they would drive to Eddie's Café for lunch. Jerilyn and Maggie soon learned that most of the people who owned and worked at the businesses were very supportive of TrailWays, some of them occasionally working there, or playing in the band that provided the music for various events.

Josh asked Jerilyn, "How about you ride with me so it will be less crowded?" And she gladly assented. Before continuing to the café, they drove by his house and the school where he taught, "just to give you an idea."

At those words, she turned to give him a glance. *An idea for what?* she wondered—that she might one day live there with him, in that house? She hardly knew him; they were just barely acquaintances. But she felt her heart leap just thinking about the possibilities. They exchanged phone numbers so they could keep in touch over the many miles which would be between them once Jerilyn returned home. And that would be soon, too soon. She was only there for a few days, and they were almost ended.

After their short trek with Austen, Jerilyn had made a few notes about things she might include in a lesson plan. But that all moved to the back of her mind after that day with Josh.

At the café, Maggie and Jerilyn watched Mark as he watched Austen. He hardly took his eyes off her, as if memorizing everything about her. Did he have any idea that his face gave away his love for her? They still didn't know the complete story. Maybe they would learn a bit more before beginning their trip back to Kansas.

Jerilyn was surprised at the sadness she felt as they drove away from TrailWays, thinking it was good Maggie was taking the first turn to drive. She couldn't remember ever being so drawn to a man. But from the time of their introduction, there had been something different, unique, special about Josh.

When plans were made to visit Austen, there was no inkling she would meet someone who would create such longing. She wasn't sure she even knew there could be such a strong emotion. But she was aching for him, and there she was in a car moving farther and farther away.

She was tempted to send a text, taking out her phone to look at his name and number—Josh Wilson.

Maggie glanced her way, sensing that Josh might be on her mind.

"Are you going to be all right?"

That simple question brought tears to her eyes. "I don't know. I have to be. He's in Nebraska. I'm in Kansas—a long way from him."

"People do move."

"I don't even know how old he is, or anything about his family."

"Does he know anything about your family, or how old you are?"

Jerilyn grinned. "No."

Feeling better, she indulged her impulse and sent a text: "We're several miles down the road toward Kansas. Maggie's driving. Glad I met you; I miss you. How old are you?" She ended with a smiling emoji and an inserted "J".

That day he met Jerilyn, Josh was shocked at his reaction. Had he ever felt that way about anyone before—even his "almost fiancée" those few years back?

When Austen mentioned some friends were coming, one a teacher, he pictured an older, plain woman, forgetting about his young female colleagues. But when he saw her and was introduced, he was immediately drawn to her—feeling an overwhelming desire to wrap her in his arms and kiss those smiling lips. He didn't feel that way about any of his fellow teachers.

It was normal for women on the trail to flirt with him, trying to catch his notice. And he usually flirted back—no harm in that. Maybe that would change since Jerilyn. Now, he realized, he felt no desire to initiate any attention from anyone else, maybe ever again.

He wished they hadn't needed to leave so soon; he wished he had spent more time with her; he wished he had learned more about her. Why hadn't he driven to TW early to tell her goodbye? At least he could have hugged her—maybe even kissed her. And why hadn't he kissed her?

Boy, Josh, you're in bad shape. Maybe you should send a text. Probably a good thing school would be starting soon. Classroom responsibilities might help keep his mind off her. Sure they would.

Then he received her text and smiled. They could keep in touch with each other, even if they weren't together.

He felt better when he responded, "So glad to hear from you. Wish I had come to tell you goodbye. I miss you too. I'm thirty-one; how old are you? J."

A return text said only: "Twenty-seven."

Later, when Austen and Mark were going through a bad time, Josh sent a message saying, "Let's don't ever be like that."

Mark and Austen, who were in a contentious relationship since their first meeting, finally came to their senses, thanks in great part to Josh's intervention. They planned a wedding to take place in just a few weeks. Josh called Jerilyn. "I know there aren't many places to stay, but if you fly, I can meet you, and you can stay in my extra room."

It took a while for Jerilyn to make a decision. She would have to take a couple of days off, not always easy for a teacher, and she wondered, "Do I know him well enough to stay with him?" Then, remembering the experience of her friend and her soon-to-be husband, she decided it could be a positive thing. At least she could become better acquainted with him, and maybe it would lead to something more than a long-distance friendship. Plus, and probably most important, there was the fact she really wanted to see him, to be with him.

So there she was on a plane headed toward Nebraska, toward him.

Since it would be a Saturday wedding, she had decided to take Friday and Monday off. As it happened, Friday was a teacher workday; so, she would miss only one day of teaching.

Josh met her at the airport with a hug and a flirty grin, then took her hand. She would have liked a kiss—and so would he.

"I'm so glad you came," he said, still holding her hand.

"Me too."

They couldn't take their eyes off each other, unaware that others in the terminal took special notice.

"Do you have other luggage?"

"No, I hope I don't need more than I could pack in this one," Jerilyn told him.

"You travel light."

"I guess so; it's easier when one travels alone."

When they were settled in his pickup, he asked, "Are you hungry?"

"Not really."

"Would you like a tour of Scottsbluff?"

"Sounds good to me."

She didn't feel any tension until they pulled into his driveway.

Josh turned to her and said, "We're here."

By the time she opened her door and got out, he was already standing beside her with her luggage, then took her hand as they walked to the door.

A thought went through her mind that this was like newlyweds returning from their honeymoon. She imagined him putting the bag down, opening the door, then picking her up in his arms to carry her across the threshold.

When she raised her eyes to his, it was like he was thinking the same thing. Was he? How could she have such vivid imaginings when there had been no kiss?

~

A female acquaintance of his, Anita O'Neill, stopped by while Jerilyn was there. The woman walked in without knocking as if that was a normal thing. She was introduced to Jerilyn, but Josh gave Anita no extra notice, making Jerilyn wonder why she was there, and why she stayed.

Anita had been a teacher at the school where he taught, then moved away. Now she was back in the area and hoped to get a position, though school was already in session. It was obvious to Jerilyn that Anita had special feelings for Josh, but she saw no indication he felt more than friendship, if even that for her; it was apparent the woman was shocked at seeing her in his house.

Anita always hoped Josh would turn to her, especially after he broke up with the woman everyone thought he was going to marry. From what she had learned from others, there was no one special for him, actually no one at all. It should be easy to get his notice. Even before leaving the area, she tried to garner his attention, hoping he would view her as more than just a fellow teacher. But Josh's only response was his usual friendly manner.

Everyone liked him; he was a favorite, popular teacher with students and parents, and well liked in town. In her imagination, Anita could picture the two of them at functions in Plattsford, gaining the notice of its citizens. She thought all that was needed was a push into closer proximity.

Then came this interloper from Kansas who was receiving more than friendly attentiveness. Watching the two, it was easy to see that Josh was attracted to Jerilyn. But that shouldn't interfere with her plans. The woman lived hundreds of miles away, though the thought that people do move passed through her mind. No one could forget the upcoming wedding of the owner of TrailWays and the woman who just happened also to be a friend of Jerilyn, who she now perceived as a rival. When Josh left the room for a while, Anita began telling Jerilyn about her relationship with him, though there wasn't one. That didn't keep her from taking every opportunity to be where he was in hopes of making it more than an imaginary connection.

~

Jerilyn was glad she came for the wedding. Mark and Austen were so happy and so much in love with each other, it almost hurt to watch them. She wondered as she glanced at Josh, would she ever have a love like that?

Jerilyn caught the bridal bouquet, then looked around to see where he was, flashing a smile when he looked at her. She held it in her hand as they danced, adding to Anita's annoyance. After a while, Kate Pearson came to take it and told her, "I'll keep it for you; don't forget to get it before you leave."

They weren't aware of the puzzled looks they were getting from most of those in attendance, wondering who the woman with Josh was? When they saw Kate take the bouquet, some speculated she might be a relative of the Pearsons.

Josh's mother was at the wedding and was curious when she saw him dancing with Jerilyn, but her son didn't usually share his personal life with her. Plus, she knew he encountered many people through the TW treks. Maybe that's where he knew her from. It never occurred to his mother that Jerilyn was the friend he said would be staying with him.

Josh later regretted not introducing the two women. That omission inadvertently led later to several months of dejection for him and for Jerilyn.

On Sunday they went to the Chimney Rock Visitors' Center, where there was a museum with exhibits, media presentations, and educational materials concerning life on the trail, as well as a museum shop. Josh suggested she might find something that could help with any lessons she would prepare for her class.

After that visit, they went to Eddie's Café for a late lunch. Several people were there who had been at the wedding the day before and watched Josh and Jerilyn as they danced. He introduced her as a friend, but they saw the way the two looked at each other.

I think I'm more than a friend, Jerilyn thought. *I hope I'm more than a friend.*

Josh's mother often ate at Eddie's. Why was he glad she wasn't there that Sunday? Why did he want to keep Jerilyn to himself with no questions and explanations? Was that why he hadn't taken her to church? Or maybe it was because he wanted to avoid another confrontation with Anita?

Jerilyn looked around as she gathered her things and packed the next morning. His extra room was a comfortable sanctuary. She decided to leave the bouquet and looked toward the dresser where she had placed it. Maybe he would think of her when he saw it.

One couldn't say that anything extraordinarily romantic occurred while she was with him, except perhaps his flirting, which was just a part of his personality, and the hugs and hand holding. And the dancing at the wedding. He pretty much flirted with everyone, except, as she remembered, there was no flirting with Maggie, who was married, nor with Austen, and not even Anita.

Besides, she loved that flirting and his smiles, and liked that he was discriminating in the choice of his attention, careful to limit it to ladies who were not in a relationship. Jerilyn knew she loved more than just his flirting. Since meeting Josh, no one drew her notice; not that they did before. She knew she had never felt like this about anyone else.

Out of necessity, Josh took Monday off from school, and now it was time to head toward the airport. She didn't want to leave, and he didn't want her to, but there was no way for that to be, at least in their minds.

The approximately thirty-mile trip to the airport was quiet. Occasionally he would reach for her hand and hold it for a while; then they were there.

He parked, carried her bag, and walked with her into the terminal. According to the overhead information, the plane would be boarding soon. Jerilyn's boarding pass was in her hand as they stood together. There were tears in her eyes and Josh's too, though she wasn't aware of it. She wanted to lean into him and have him hold her and ask her not to go. At the very least, she wanted a kiss. None of that happened, only a quick hug.

"I'm so glad you came."

"Me too."

The same words as those when she arrived.

"Take care, call when you get home."

"I will; keep in touch."

Then she was walking down the runway—away from him.

Neither of them had any idea as to what was going to transpire in the next few months. Otherwise, maybe it would have been a different parting.

Two

It was during that trip for Mark and Austen's wedding when Jerilyn heard Kate Pearson say, "It's about time."

She said it; and nearly everyone at the wedding could have echoed it as they thought back over the entire summer the two wasted before finally admitting their love for each other.

Several weeks after she returned home, she began to think that sentiment also applied to her and Josh. Would there ever be a time for them? Their relationship was not contentious, but what was it? They had established a special friendship—relationship, or whatever it was—almost immediately. And it grew in the rare times they were together. For a while, they exchanged texts and phone calls before they tapered off. Then silence—no texts, no phone calls. Was it her fault or his? Had they both become so busy with school, there was no time for anything else?

When she missed him most, she scrolled through her texts to read them again. There was a special one she read over and over.

"Hi. My house feels so empty without you. And so does my heart. Wish we weren't so far apart. Texts and phone calls are great, but not very satisfying in the long run. School is good; kids keep me focused. Hope all is well with you."

She didn't know he did the same.

"Hello. So glad to get your texts. Though I love hearing your voice, I can always read your texts again. Wish I could have stayed with you longer. Wish you weren't so far away. School's okay. Take care."

~

Much time had passed since those texts were sent. Thanksgiving had been celebrated. Christmas decorations were in the stores, carols on the radio.

A new teacher at her school had wasted no time in pursuing Jerilyn, and she let him. At least that's the way she thought of it. She liked him, but was unable to develop a stronger emotion than that. There was no one she was attracted to, and it was nice having someone to squire her around to places she wanted and needed to go so she wouldn't always be alone.

Jerilyn didn't mention to Austen, nor to anyone, including her group of church friends, her feelings for Josh. Though Maggie had a good idea because she was there and saw them together. So, when she was seen with Derek Ireland, they passed that information along.

Merritt Long was one friend who had originally planned to make the trip with them, but decided not to, expecting she would see Austen after Labor Day.

In one text to Austen, she said, "Wish I would have made the trip with Maggie and Jerilyn so I could have met your Mr. Thomas. Will you be coming home to Overland Park any time soon? A new teacher at Jerilyn's school has really been rushing her. Seems that if anything is happening, they are there together."

Austen received similar information from others, and only later, wondered why Jerilyn never mentioned him. And why didn't she ask Jerilyn about it before texting her about seeing Josh and Anita together?

There was one she especially regretted sending: "Seems like anywhere Josh is these days, so is Anita. Looks like they might become a couple after all. I also note she spends a lot of time with his mother." Sadly, she didn't notice it was always Anita making all the moves.

Thus, the early communication between the two tapered to nothing, each believing the other was in a relationship with someone else. Austen would mention him occasionally when she called, giving little information about what Jerilyn really wanted to know.

So the months passed with both Jerilyn and Josh reluctant to make a move to learn for themselves. They cared so much for the other, they didn't want to create a situation that might generate dissatisfaction. Somehow their friends and families missed how despondent and dejected they both were during the holidays.

But Mark did know differently, at least as far as Josh was concerned. Perhaps because of his early relationship, or non-relationship with Austen. Josh seemed to be slowly losing interest in everything, occasionally asking Mark if Austen ever heard anything from Jerilyn, telling him, "I would call, but I don't want to interfere in her life. I want her to be happy. Besides, I'm not sure how I would feel, hearing her voice and not being able to touch her. And knowing she was with someone else."

When Mark mentioned Josh's unhappiness to Austen and what initiated it, she felt bad, and the two of them started discussing what they might be able to do to alleviate the situation.

They were planning a trip to visit her parents and former in-laws, and while they were there would go through the storage shed where she put her things before she left for Nebraska. They would rent a truck to carry back to Trail-Ways whatever they decided to take.

Spring break for school was several weeks away, but knowing when it was, and that Josh was always ready to be of assistance, they decided to make their trip at that time and ask him to join them to help on the drive back. Austen was pregnant and not feeling well. If Josh helped, not only would she be relieved of the long drive, but she and David would be able to stay with her parents a bit longer, then fly home.

As they expected, Josh was happy to make the trip. At the same time, he hoped he would get a chance to see Jerilyn again, not knowing she thought he and Anita were a couple. Her spring break was at the same time, and she looked forward to a visit with Austen. They even planned a get-together with their church group one afternoon to catch up on each other's lives.

It was the same afternoon that Josh flew in, so he was at the Morgans' when Jerilyn brought Austen home. He and Mark planned to pack up the things to be moved the next day, then begin the long journey to Nebraska early the following morning. When the two women walked in together, Josh was standing with his back to the door and Jerilyn didn't realize he was there until she reached him and touched his shoulder, thinking it was Mark. "Hey, so glad to see you."

Josh turned at that, and gave her a hug, holding her for a while. He said, "Glad to see you too." Then there was that grin that created butterflies in her stomach, just as his cowboy hat tilted over his bright blue eyes always did.

"I didn't expect to see you," Jerilyn told him. "What are you doing here?" *I thought I was over any feelings for him, but here they are. What am I going to do about it? How can I stand going through that again?*

"Looks like I'm going to get to have the same experience you did, driving from here to the Nebraska Panhandle. We're going to load the truck tomorrow; maybe you'd like to come help?"

Austen told Jerilyn, "I'm going to be there to make sure they take everything I want. So why don't you come? David will stay here with my folks while we're busy doing that."

Jerilyn felt somewhat guilty about it, believing that Josh was in a serious relationship, but agreed anyway.

Mark said, "It's still early," then, turning to Jerilyn, "Why don't you give Josh a tour of your city? He's asked lots of questions I can't answer, and I want Austen to rest." Then with a grin, said, "We're ordering pizza later, so you can join us."

Nothing like putting her on the spot, and in a dilemma. She wanted to be with Josh but wasn't sure she could stand being alone with him in close proximity, believing it would be just a one-time occurrence.

Watching Mark and Austen together created a great longing in her. Jerilyn determined she would never marry unless she found that kind of love; she wanted a man she adored, and one who adored her. Knowing she would never feel that way about her fellow teacher, she needed to stop leaning on him and give him a chance to find someone who would.

She was also afraid Josh might be that person for her. What was she going to do to be able to bear that knowledge? Driving in the car with him would surely add to her disconsolate feelings, but what excuse could she use to avoid it happening?

A few minutes passed after Mark's suggestion, and Jerilyn realized they were all watching, waiting for her to respond. Putting a smile on, she said, "Okay, let's go. It's a spread-out city, but I can at least show you some popular sites."

Jerilyn backed her car into the street, then began her spiel. "Overland Park wasn't incorporated until 1960, and at that time the population was only about 25,000. Now it's grown to almost 200,000. My grandparents moved here a couple of years later, when my grandfather was hired for the police department. I think he was the twenty-sixth officer."

Josh stopped her after that information, saying, "I don't really want a tour of the city. I'd like to see where you live, maybe the school where you teach, maybe meet your parents. We can save the tour for another time."

Where did that come from? He wanted to know her family but wasn't intending for it to be voiced just yet. His statement also surprised Jerilyn; what did it mean? If he were serious about another woman, why would he want to know more about her? And what did he mean by another time? Was it just to be polite?

"That's easy. My mom died a couple of years ago, but I'll check with my dad to see if he's home and ready for visitors. My brothers might be there too."

Her family's home was south of the Morgans', and not too far from hers. Her dad was glad to have company and met them at the door when they arrived. Jerilyn had said little about her trip to visit Austen, and even less about Josh. But he recalled the lilt in her voice when she mentioned him. It was necessary for Josh to remove his hat when in her car, but he put it on as he climbed out. She noticed that the young woman who lived next door was checking her flower beds and turned to give him a second look. Yes, he appealed to her too, with his cowboy boots and hat.

"Josh Wilson, this is my dad Jefferson Tate, though everyone knows him as Jeff."

The two men shook hands, each taking measure of the other. She wasn't aware of it, but her dad looked at Josh as a potential son-in-law, while Josh thought Jeff might someday be his father-in-law. Each was well impressed with the other man.

"Your brothers may be by later," her dad said. "They were busy with some important project this morning, but come on in. I have a loaf of banana bread someone gave me recently, and I can make coffee."

"The Morgans are going to order pizza—a favorite meal for their grandson David. But a slice of banana bread shouldn't spoil our appetite," Jerilyn said, glancing at Josh.

Josh nodded with that grin of his, and added, "A cup of coffee would go well with it."

The bread and coffee were good, and they had a friendly visit, though her brothers never came. Josh said, "Maybe next time."

There were those words again, as if he were expecting to be here at a later time, a next time.

When they were back in the car, Josh asked her what her brothers' names were. "Jon—or Jonson, and Jack—or Jackson," Jerilyn said. "My mother was Joyce, so you can see there was somewhat of a pattern; our names all begin with "J." And before you ask, I have no idea where Jerilyn came from. Maybe it was in some book my mother read once."

"Then I would fit right in with my 'J'," Josh said.

Why had that not occurred to her? The thought created a knot in her stomach. What was he trying to say, that he expected, wanted, hoped to be part of her family?

To change the subject, Jerilyn asked, "What about your family? How is it I didn't meet any of them when I was there?" Then she wondered if she would have remembered. *Josh was so much on my mind.*

"There's my mother, and one sister. Actually, my mother stopped by that day you met Anita, but she didn't come in; and she was even at the wedding, but I didn't get a chance to introduce you."

Talk about a dash, or more accurately, a bucket, of cold water. Just when she was beginning to believe there might be a chance after all for them to be a couple, she was reminded of the other woman.

As that thought was going through her mind, Josh got a text saying the pizza would arrive soon.

Jerilyn was glad there was not time to show him either her home or school. Especially her home—she wouldn't be able to bear being in it later, knowing he was once there, but probably never again.

"Sorry we have to cut the tour short," she said.

"Maybe next time," he answered.

Those words again. "Why do you keep talking as if there's going to be a next time?"

Josh replied, "Because I'm hoping there will be."

They reached the Morgans', so no more chance to pursue the subject. Jerilyn thought seriously about not going in but knew that would be cowardly. What was that word Austen mentioned to her? Pusillanimous? Yes, that fit exactly how she was feeling.

Everyone was at the table, waiting with two empty chairs side by side. When Jerilyn chose one, Josh helped her get it adjusted, then took his seat beside her. The others noticed his special attention to her, though she seemed oblivious of it, and made note of the picture the two made: Josh's blonde, wavy hair, and blue eyes, and Jerilyn's auburn hair and brown eyes.

Standing behind her before he took his seat, Josh felt an overwhelming desire to kiss the back of Jerilyn's neck. Why was he being so reticent? To the best of his memory, she was the only woman who had ever affected him that way. In the past, he would have gone for the kiss and thought nothing about it, but she was special, and he didn't want to make any mistakes. He settled for squeezing her shoulders; in response she turned, raised her eyes to his, and smiled as he did. It was a while before the connection was broken. He felt his heart beating faster, as was hers. How could she not respond to that smile, those flirty eyes?

Josh's agreement to help Mark and Austen was partly, maybe mostly, in the hope or expectation of seeing Jerilyn, and now he was acting like some shy youth on his first date.

When all were settled, Richard Morgan said grace, with David adding, "Thank you, God, for the pizza."

Jerilyn was glad she stayed; there was much conversation about what was happening at TrailWays and the two almost-newlyweds who were expecting. She asked, "Do you know whether it's a boy or girl? Do you want to know?"

Mark and Austen smiled at each other, then told her they were waiting, not wanting to know until the birth. David knew there was a baby on the way and was excited to be a big brother in a few months. Not that he understood completely. They did mention that a boy would be named Richard and a girl would be Morgan, explaining to Josh and Jerilyn that the Richard was not only for Austen's dad, but Mark's mother, whose maiden name was Richards. Morgan, of course, was for Austen's maiden name, just as she was named for her mother.

At the explanation of the names, Josh and Jerilyn glanced at each other, smiling, remembering their recent conversation about names. Then he said to her, "Maybe your dad can tell you the origin of your name."

They may have already known, but for Mark's benefit, he told those around the table: "All of her family have names beginning with the letter 'J.'"

To which Mark replied, "Then you would fit right in."

Austen noticed that Jerilyn's face fell at that statement, wondering what that meant, and how it might affect their plans for the next morning.

Jerilyn finally said, "It's getting late, and if you want me to help tomorrow, I need to get home and into bed."

So that question was answered.

Only Josh responded, saying, "I want you."

Jerilyn wondered if anyone else noticed the innuendo. On one hand, she liked it, but what did it really mean in the end? He walked her to her car, telling her, "I enjoyed the tour, short as it was. Glad I got to meet your dad. See you tomorrow." And again, a quick hug.

Josh stood watching until her car was out of sight, and again, wondering what the wisdom was of pursuing a long-distance relationship. But how could he not; he knew he was falling in love with her, if not already fallen. Seeing her again only made it more obvious. And though she was surprised at seeing him, she seemed to be happy about it, convincing him there was hope.

Three

Jerilyn arrived at the Morgans' at nine o'clock the next morning, and then she and Austen used her car to drive to the storage complex. Mr. Morgan drove the guys to the rental place to pick up the truck Mark had reserved.

It was a little less than a year since Austen had put her things in storage, but now it seemed like a lifetime, because there had been so many changes. She planned to take most of the furniture, but was most unsure about the desk that she and David's dad had restored that was almost a twin to one in Mark's house. And that restoration had been a lifetime ago—David's lifetime. They had finished it just a few weeks before his birth. Then his dad died only six months later. That happy time changed into sadness very quickly.

Mark noticed her tears and came to wrap her in the sanctuary of his arms, recognizing the opposing emotions she was feeling.

"Oh, Mark, I'm sorry," she said as she leaned into him. "I love you so much; I'm so glad I met you. But that time was my life and I thought it would always be my life. And long ago as it was, I feel grief. Maybe I didn't do all my grieving then. Instead I had to face what my new life was going to be, and deal with that."

"And I'm sorry you had to deal with that sadness," Mark replied. "I have mixed feelings too. If not for that, we would never have met, and I wouldn't have you and David to love. No question, we have to take the desk for David."

A few more minutes in Mark's arms, and she was ready to continue with the sorting. She chose to take most of David's and her clothes to go through later when there would be more time. He had probably outgrown most of his, but if her baby was a boy, they might be able to use some of them.

There was much to load into the truck. And as she went through her things, she was reminded of how the pioneers must have felt when they were preparing to travel to Oregon, and then later needed to discard so much. At least she wouldn't have to do that.

~

The four went for lunch, and when they returned to the storage shed, it took little time to finish loading the truck. Having completed the job earlier than expected, Mark and Josh discussed starting on the trip to Nebraska instead of waiting 'til the next day so they could get in a few hours of driving before dark. Whatever their decision, they would need to drive back to the Morgans' anyway to get their clothes. Mark asked Austen what she thought. There had been no separation since their marriage, and both were dreading the trip because of that, no matter when it was.

"I'll worry until we're back together, but it could be a good thing. You may even get home before dark tomorrow," Austen told him. They gazed into each other's eyes, almost sadly.

Then Mark said, "Okay, let's get started," he said to Josh, "We'll meet you girls back at the Morgans'."

David was upset that Mark was leaving and began to cry. "It's okay, cowboy, we'll be together again in just a few days. Be sure to take good care of Mommie 'til then."

They held hands, making a circle as Richard Morgan offered a prayer, thanking God for all the blessings He had given and asking for a safe journey for the men as they traveled to Nebraska. Squeezing hands, they all added their amens.

Then after giving a loving hug to the boy, Mark reached for Austen. They stood with their arms around each other for some time before their kiss. Anyone watching could see it was an emotional time for them; it was hard for Josh and Jerilyn to watch, and Jerilyn thought, *That's what I want.*

Later, she wasn't sure if it was that picture of love or something else, but Josh came to her, his hat in his hand as he wrapped her in his arms. Jerilyn's went around him in a long embrace, then almost naturally but unexpectedly, they too kissed. It was to have been just an "I'm glad you were here; I'll miss you kiss," but at the first touch of their lips, it became so much more. He pulled her closer for a deeper, more fulfilling one, saying, "I've wanted to kiss you since I first saw you."

She felt the same way, though a kiss didn't necessarily need to mean anything. People kissed nowadays for the same reasons they used to shake hands. But this one didn't feel like that. She would remember it forever. She was glad he gave no apology, just a sweet smile.

Then Josh told her, "It's been so good to see you again. I'll miss you."

"Me too."

With his hat back on his head, he cupped her face in his hands, gave her one last quick kiss, then climbed into the passenger seat of the truck. She didn't see the tears in his eyes, nor he hers, each wondering when they might see each other again. She said a silent prayer asking God to bring her the man He had chosen for her; and if it was Josh, to give her the patience she needed to wait.

Josh and Jerilyn were so focused on each other they weren't aware that Austen noticed that first kiss, and with a finger over her lips to stop Mark from saying anything, she took a picture.

Jerilyn, Austen, and David waved until the truck was out of sight; and though they couldn't see them, Mark and Josh kept their eyes on the trio, watching from the rearview mirrors.

~

Austen was going to take David to see his Wiley grandparents the next day. She tried to keep in regular touch with them, and sent pictures chronicling his growth. He had recently celebrated his fifth birthday, and she mentioned that when she got home, one of the first things she needed to do was get him enrolled in school.

The Wileys had attended her wedding, but that was months ago, and they were especially eager to see their grandson again. She hadn't told them of her pregnancy, so was somewhat anxious as to how they would react.

~

Jerilyn climbed into her car and sat for a while before leaving. Thinking of the unexpected emotional day with a first kiss, maybe with the man she was to spend the rest of her life with. But how could that happen? They lived so far apart, and there didn't seem to be any uncomplicated way they could change that. Saying, "God, I leave it in your hands," she started the car and backed out of the driveway.

Loath to head home yet, she called her dad to see if he was home. They hadn't talked since she and Josh had been there, and she wondered what he thought about the man.

"Sure, come on by. Your brothers are here too."

Almost as soon as Jerilyn got in the door, her dad said, "I liked that young man you brought by here—Josh?"

"Yes, Josh. He liked you too."

"So, what's the story with you two? I noticed you could hardly keep your eyes off each other. Not like that Derek guy you've brought by a couple of times."

She was surprised at his question, since she wasn't aware they had been so focused on each other.

"Since you ask," Jerilyn told him, "you know we live hundreds of miles apart, and I can't see that we will ever have more than a long-distance friendship."

Her dad countered with, "Doesn't have to be that way. If you figure out that you love each other, then you'll figure out how to solve the problem."

Love, even her father believed in it. By then they were in the kitchen, where her brothers were listening closely to the conversation.

Jon said, "We heard about that guy from Nebraska. How well do you know him? Is he more than just a hand at that TrailWays place?"

Both of her brothers were younger, but still took a protective stance toward her. Jerilyn wished they would find serious girlfriends and protect them instead of her. Jon had recently completed his firefighter training and Jack was almost finished with the Police Academy.

"Josh is a sixth-grade teacher. During the last several years, he has served as the Pony Express Rider for TrailWays during the summer season. And I guess I must admit, I don't really know him very well; I've only seen him about five or six times. But if you must know, I like him very much and wish we didn't live so far apart. I've enjoyed every one of those times more than I can explain."

"So how about you two? Have you found anyone special yet?" They looked at each other and grinned, thinking their sister was trying to change the subject. She was good at that.

"Whatcha gonna do about Derek?"

The ball was back in her court, and she had no answer.

Mark and Josh were silent as they started down the street, heading the several miles toward I-29, which would lead them north to intersect with a smaller highway in Nebraska.

When they were well on their way, Mark said, "That was quite a kiss back there."

Josh gave him a startled look. His mind wasn't on the others when he finally kissed Jerilyn. There had been so many times when he wanted to, when no one else was around. Now he wondered if it would be the only kiss.

Mark continued, "So what's gonna happen now? Do you know she thinks you're in a serious relationship?"

"No—who?" Josh asked.

"Anita."

Josh wondered, "Why would she think that?"

"Plenty of things that have been intimated, misinterpreted, and whatever women feel." Mark told him, "It's even possible that Austen and I have contributed to that, from things we observed. I'm sorry about that. And you have to admit, Anita takes every opportunity to insert herself into your life, even if you've done nothing to encourage it."

"It doesn't matter," Josh said. "Jerilyn has a boyfriend anyway."

"I believe he's just a friend who happens to be male. I've seen the way you look at her, and the way she looks at you. Don't waste time like I did," Mark advised him.

"But we live so far apart," Josh said, almost sadly. "How can we have more than a long-distance friendship?"

"Think, man: we have planes and automobiles. Sorry, no trains out in the panhandle, except maybe coal trains, nor wagon trains now, not even going back after seeing the elephant, but there's a way. Don't settle for less than the best life; you and she can figure it out."

Josh asked, "Did you exaggerate Austen's health problem to get me to come, so I could see Jerilyn again?"

"What do you think?"

"Yeah, you two fought it for months for whatever reason," Josh reminded him.

"I thought it was a good reason," Mark told him. "Don't make that mistake."

"Talk about stubborn. Everybody knew you were crazy about each other."

"Yeah," said Mark. "Don't think I ever thanked you for pushing me that day, finally getting some sense in my stubborn head."

"You probably just didn't want to be called Stupid," Josh said.

"Do you?"

There was no answer from Josh. Was he being stupid, or was it wise not to hope too much?

"Okay, I'll leave it alone, at least for a while," Mark said. "When we turn west into Nebraska, we'll be getting closer to Lincoln. We can take a couple of smaller highways to get there. Not sure how long that will take, but the hours and miles are passing. Plus, we'll be headed into the setting sun. Think I'll check with Matt to see if we can go by there, maybe spend the night. What do you think?"

"Sounds good to me," Josh replied. "Will be good to see Peggy and Patsy too."

~

Jerilyn stared at her brothers, then said, "I don't know what I'm going to do about Derek. I do like him, but don't believe

I could ever feel about him the way I already do for Josh. No, I know I can't. So, yes, it's not fair to him if he might be thinking there could be a future for us."

Then Jon asked, "What do you know about Linda?"

"Linda?"

"Yeah—Austen's sister," he told her.

The question had more than surprised her. She wasn't aware that either of her brothers knew Linda.

"I may not know any more than you do. She hasn't been around more than a few times when I've been with Austen or the Morgans. She's been a flight attendant for a few years and so does a lot of traveling. I believe she was even on international flights for a while. How long have you known her?"

"Probably can't say I know her. Remember the Open House at the fire station a few weeks ago? She was there with her folks; they introduced us."

"Nothing since then?"

With a grin, Jon said, "Well I did find out she likes this particular band—so checked when and where they might be appearing. I happened to be off, so stopped by mostly to see if she was there. She was."

"And?" Jerilyn prompted.

"She was with a group, guys and girls; I didn't know any of them, though some looked familiar. I learned later they were in a young singles group at church. I've thought about becoming part of that group, but my strange work hours pretty much prevented it. Though I suppose I could still participate part of the time."

"Did you join them that time?" Jerilyn asked.

"Oh, yeah, though I didn't really know them, they all seemed to recognize me. They made room, leaving a chair across from Linda. We all talked a lot, enjoyed the band, then went our separate ways. None seemed to be in a special relationship."

"So, did you talk to Linda?"

"Only in the group," Jon told her. "And, no, I don't have a phone number."

"Guess you could always stop by the Morgans to see if she's there, or maybe get her number from them?"

Her brother admitted, "Don't think I want to be that forward."

"Well, it's your life. But I would think a brave firefighter could be that forward," Jerilyn said, grinning.

At Jerilyn's questioning look, Jack said, "No, no one special. Guess I'm having too much fun playing the field."

Jon grinned as if he knew something Jack wasn't admitting.

She forgot about her plan to ask her father about the origin of her name, and, telling them all, "Bye, I love you," left for her home.

~

After spending the night with his brother Matt and family, Mark and Josh were now on I-80 getting closer to home, but still with many miles in front of them.

Both were thinking of the women they had left in Kansas when Josh said, "Man, just think, our girls drove this route. They're tough."

"Yes, and stubborn and committed and beautiful. So, what are you going to do about Jerilyn and your future?"

"Don't know yet about Jerilyn. Sure wish she didn't live so far away. But I have been thinking about my future; actually, have been for a while," Josh told him. "Think I'm going to check into what I need regarding college hours and other qualifications to become a school principal. If I ever get married, that would probably be a good thing. I've heard that some school districts don't seriously consider a single man in that position."

Just then he received a text, and looking at the name of the sender, a grin spread across his face. Mark didn't even ask who it was from, knowing by Josh's reaction it was Jerilyn.

Mark called Austen just before they climbed in the truck for the final part of the journey, wanting to hear her voice. He was surprised how he felt about this small separation that would be only for a couple of days.

"I miss you; are you feeling okay, taking care of yourself? Who will take you to the airport?" he asked.

"The Wileys asked if they could take us, and I agreed. They miss being able to see David and may plan to come visit this summer. And I miss you too; hope you are being careful. I'm glad you stopped last night, so you'll be rested for your trip today. I love you, Mr. Thomas."

"I love you too; can't wait 'til we're together again, Mrs. Thomas."

~

Josh had texted Jerilyn to tell her they were stopping in Lincoln for the night. It seemed to her as if they were already separated by more than miles. Texts were not very satisfying, but she didn't believe she could stand hearing his voice in a phone call, knowing she couldn't see him, couldn't touch him. What were they going to do about their relationship? Though he admitted he had wanted to kiss her, there were no words indicating he might be interested in anything permanent.

When Jerilyn arrived home the night before, her house somehow felt empty, though before these recent times with Josh, it had always felt cozy, comfortable, and restful.

Before she did anything else the next morning, she texted Josh, letting him know how much she had enjoyed the time with him, and hoped he and Mark would have a safe trip and reach home before it was too late. Then she asked him to keep in touch.

Texting back, Josh told her, "You too. I missed our texts and phone calls. I care about only you. Remember that."

Four

Derek had gone out of town for spring break and didn't know about Josh's visit and the time Jerilyn spent with him. Actually, he knew nothing about Josh at all. Jerilyn found no reason to mention him, probably because she wanted to keep everything about Josh to herself. And there were no thoughts about Derek for days, until her brothers brought up his name. Thus, she wasn't prepared when she got a call from him the day after Josh left.

"Hi, Jer, I'm back in town. Missed you while I was gone; did you miss me?"

Jer. How had she not noticed that before? She didn't like the shortening of her name; was Derek the only one who used it? And had that been true since they first met? She loved how her name came from Josh's lips—"Jerilyn"—almost an endearment.

"Jer, are you still there?"

"Oh, yes, I guess," Jerilyn answered. "My friend Austen and her husband were in town. They came to get her things from storage. It was good to see her. It was a wonderful visit. She's expecting in October."

She sounded distracted, not like the Jer he knew, her words clipped and cryptic. Did something happen? Maybe it was just having visited with her good friend, then having her leave again. He knew that Austen was a special friend and Jerilyn missed her.

"Okay, just wondering if you'd like to go to dinner this evening?" Derek asked. "Maybe we can get caught up before starting school again."

Jerilyn didn't want to; it would be a reminder that Josh was gone, not here, maybe never would be again, though he had mentioned "next time" more than once. She wasn't ready to see Derek; what did they have to get caught up on? Still, she agreed to go. "Will you pick me up?"

He answered with, "How about you meet me at Cinzetti's at six o'clock?"

"Okay."

Not okay. Why couldn't he pick her up, so she didn't have to drive? Thinking back, there were many times that Jerilyn met him somewhere. That should make it easier when she told him there was someone else for her.

Except for the few tears she shed as the truck carrying Josh drove off, she had not cried, but then she did. She felt broken, empty, lost, needing a hug, but wanting it only from Josh. Why had he come? Why did she let him kiss her? Why did she kiss him back? Looking to the future, she could see only vacant days, weeks, even years, ahead, despite the words they'd exchanged. Words were easy. Doing was something completely different. What was her thought those months ago—that it was a journey? Would it always be that way?

Could she bear the times between any visits? Would there be a happy ending, and if so, how long would it be before that happened?

~

When their spring break began, Anita headed south to visit a friend and enjoy the somewhat warmer weather and sunshine than they currently had in Nebraska. She texted Josh several times and even tried to call him once, to no avail, making her wonder if he might have lost his phone.

When she returned to Nebraska, after calling once more, she decided to drive by his home. His pickup wasn't there, so maybe he was out of town too; though that still didn't answer the question of why there was no response to any of her attempts to contact him. Not that it was usual for them to keep in touch. Still in her car, Anita called his mother.

"Hello, Anita, how nice to hear from you."

"Hi, Mrs. Wilson."

"Mattie, please."

"Okay, Mattie. I've been out of town and Josh hasn't answered any of my texts or calls. Just wondering if he's okay?"

"Oh yes," his mother said. "I'm surprised he didn't tell you," still not realizing that Josh would have felt no reason to let Anita know. "Mark and Austen flew back to Kansas to move her things out of storage. Did you know she's pregnant?" she asked. "After they got there, Mark decided he didn't want her to have to make that long ride back in the truck they rented. So he contacted Josh to ask if he could fly in and drive back with him, leaving Austen and David to fly back later.

"They're on the road now," she added. "Spent a night in Lincoln with Matt—you know that's Mark's brother? Will probably be driving in later today."

"Will he need a ride to Scottsbluff to pick up his truck?"

"I don't know," Mattie replied. "Someone from Trail-Ways may have taken him."

Mattie welcomed the words from Anita. She seemed like a nice girl. She even sat with her sometimes at church. Though, thinking about it further, not when Josh was there. Still, in his mother's mind, it was about time for Josh to get married, and she thought Anita could be the one for him. She had not met Jerilyn and knew nothing of their relationship, had no idea that a woman in Kansas might be special to her son.

Anita was continuing to cultivate her relationship with Josh's mother, even though she wasn't sure whether she liked Mrs. Wilson or not.

"I'll text him to find out," Anita told her. "Maybe he'll answer this time."

Josh groaned and winced when he saw who'd sent the text.

"What's wrong, bad news?" Mark asked.

"Maybe. It's Anita again."

Once more he chose not to answer. Anita thought nothing of it, believing they might be in an area where he couldn't receive service. It didn't occur to her that he may have seen Jerilyn when he was in Kansas. Even if his mother didn't know of his feelings for Jerilyn, she did, and would do everything she could to help him forget about 'the other woman', not realizing that it didn't make a difference, would never make a difference, regardless of what happened between him and Jerilyn.

Another text, and Josh was glad to see it was from his mother.

"I just had a call from Anita. She's worried about not hearing from you. Sure seems like a nice girl."

He replied, "I need to tell you about Jerilyn," adding nothing else, and not responding to her reference to Anita.

"Jerilyn?"

"Yes, Mom. I'll tell you everything when I'm home. We're making good progress, so that should be just a few more hours."

"Will you need a ride to the airport to get your pickup?"

"No, it's at TW. Bill took me to the airport."

She asked, "What if Anita calls again?"

"Tell her whatever you want," Josh replied. "But don't encourage her."

Jerilyn called her Small Group leader before going to Cinzetti's, confirming when they were to meet again. She needed the positive feelings and affirmations that were always part of their sessions. And especially now, she needed the love of the group. She hadn't shared her feelings for Josh with them, though Maggie West was with her when she met him, so she knew. As she'd thought, they were to meet in a couple of days. She asked the leader to specifically pray for the despondency she was experiencing.

She dreaded the upcoming meeting with Derek, but perhaps it was good to do so while her time with Josh was so fresh. Regardless of what might ultimately happen with him, there was no wish for a future with Derek, and he needed to know so he could use his time finding someone who did.

Now might be a good time to investigate requirements to be a special education teacher, something she had thought about for a while. Maybe she could start evening classes if she needed more hours and have something new to occupy her mind.

She checked the time and realized she needed to head to Cinzetti's, though she wasn't looking forward to it. She liked the place; in fact, it was a favorite location for her group of church friends to meet. She hoped this upcoming meeting with Derek wouldn't spoil that.

They were escorted to a table and told the special menu items of the day. Both were there often, and pretty much knew what they were going to choose from the buffet, whether they were specials or not. After filling their plates, as they took their seats, Jerilyn was pondering how to introduce the subject of their relationship.

Derek opened up with, "We've been seeing each other for a while. We get along pretty well, and I'm thinking maybe we should take it up a notch."

That was unexpected. Where did that notion come from? She couldn't remember any time there was any indication that their relationship would ever be more than just an occasion to attend certain work-associated events together. She knew there were no kisses. Had they even held hands? There had been no kisses with Josh until a few days ago—or was it only yesterday? But at least there was his flirting, and hers, and she smiled as she thought about him. Would she have reacted differently to Derek's statement before seeing and being with—and even kissing Josh?

Derek saw the smile and interpreted it to mean she was open to what was on his mind, so he continued, "We get along well, have the same kind of job, and, I think, have the same interests."

She gave him a piercing look, then asked, "And you think that's enough to, as you say, 'take it up a notch'?"

He told her, "Sure, I think that's the main thing in a serious relationship."

"What about love, or at least affection?" Jerilyn felt herself shrinking away from him.

"Yeah, they're important, but that can come later, as we get to know each other better," he said almost smilingly, as if there was no question that would happen.

Getting to know each other better sounded almost like an arranged relationship.

"I'm sorry, Derek, the only reason I came tonight was to let you know that from my viewpoint, our association has gone as far as it's going to go. And for me, love is the most important ingredient in a relationship. In my view, it must be there before considering making it permanent. I should have been honest with you from the start. I love a man who I've only seen a few times; and no, he isn't from here. But he was here for a few days recently, and that love became even more obvious."

Getting up, she left some money on the table and said, "I can't stay. I guess I'll see you at school in a couple of days."

Having admitted her love for Josh, even if he didn't know it, she texted him as soon as she arrived home.

"You're probably home, or almost home by now. Hope all has gone well; I've decided I'm going to check into requirements for a special education teacher. Maybe I'll be attending classes at night. Please keep in touch."

When Josh received the text, he was relieved and happy to see that it was from Jerilyn. Though she didn't say it, he felt she sent it because she was missing him as he was missing her. How could that be? It had hardly been a day since they were together, but there were now so many miles between them.

"Yes, we're almost home," he texted. "Wish you were here. I'm thinking of checking into what's needed to become a school principal. May be taking courses this summer instead of riding for the Pony Express. How about that? I'll try to call you tomorrow." And he wanted to add, "I love you," but didn't.

Remembering he needed to talk to his mother about Jerilyn, he called her. "Hi, Mom, we're pulling into TrailWays now. Really tired; I'll have to come back tomorrow to help Mark move the things out of the truck and put them wherever we're going to put them. But I need to see you; is it okay if I stop by early in the morning?"

"I'm glad you're back home, and of course, I'm always glad to see you, whatever time. Why don't you plan to come for breakfast—seven o'clock?"

~

Josh's heart started beating more rapidly as soon as he heard Jerilyn's voice. "Hello, are you home?"

"Yes, it was a tiring trip. Probably like yours was when you made your trip last summer. We were both glad to get here. I know Mark can hardly wait until Austen and David are home again," Josh said. "And I miss you. Going to have breakfast with my mother tomorrow. Going to tell her about you. I should have a long time ago. Guess I wanted you to be my secret love."

"We have a lot to think about," Jerilyn said. "I miss you."

Just a few more words from each, and they said goodbye. Neither wanted to end the call, both continuing to hold their phones. But that was the way their life was going to be—for a while, at least.

~

As the call ended, there was a visit from Anita. First thing she said was, "I sure missed you over break. Was glad to get away. I heard you helped Mark move Austen's things back here. Did you do anything else interesting?"

When had she started just walking into his house? He should have noticed it before and stopped it. *I need to start locking my doors.* With no lead up to what he was going to say, he told her, "Yes, took the trip to Kansas to help Mark and Austen, and got to see Jerilyn."

For a while, the name meant nothing to her, then she remembered the interloper from Kansas.

"So—how is she?"

"She's wonderful, sweet, and beautiful, and I hope to marry her." Josh didn't plan to say all that, but there it was, and it was how he felt. And why did he say it to Anita and not the woman he loved? Regardless of everything, he didn't want to be like Mark, who took so long to admit his feelings.

"Marry? But you hardly know her, and she lives so far away."

Anita could think of nothing else to say. She knew of Josh's special feelings for the Kansas woman, but still thought because of the distance between them, he would eventually turn to her, because she was there.

"Yes, she is, but we'll overcome that obstacle. And if I'm honest, I've wanted her to be mine since I first saw her," Josh admitted. "It doesn't always take time."

It was hard for her to accept; she should have known. Despite all her efforts to make their connection special, there was never any encouragement from him. The rest of the school year was going to be hard, seeing him every day. But there was still that separation, and she and Josh were still here in the same town.

Five

"Morning, Mom," Josh said, giving Mrs. Wilson a hug.

"And to you, son," his mother replied. "So glad you could come for breakfast. I don't see you enough and kind of feel like I'm missing out on things happening in your life."

"Yeah, I know I haven't been good at sharing, so it's my fault when there are times you don't know what's important to me. And what's not."

His mother filled a plate and set it in front of him, then took one for herself before sitting down.

"Okay, who is Jerilyn? And why haven't you mentioned her before? I thought Anita was an important part of your life—but she isn't?" Mrs. Wilson asked.

"It's Anita who's tried to convince you she's an important part of my life," Josh told her. "Do you remember before Anita left—whenever that was—she was, for lack of a better word, chasing me? I didn't like it then, and I like it even less now. And I'm sorry, Mom, but your paying attention to Anita has encouraged her.

"Jerilyn is a friend of Austen." His mother noticed the way he said the name, as if she were with him, and he wanted to embrace her. "She was here a few days last summer. That's when we met. And though it was only a couple of days, it was enough for me to know I wanted her to be a special part of my life. I'm pretty sure she felt the same way. And Jerilyn is the friend who came for the wedding and stayed with me. Don't know how I missed introducing you," Josh told her. "Think I was afraid to expose my feelings. You probably didn't even know the friend was female.

"Besides that," he continued, "even though Jerilyn was at my house, Anita seemed to always be there. Jerilyn is a teacher too and could only take a couple of days off. I didn't want to share that time."

"Oh, Josh, I'm so sorry if I've made your life more complicated than it needs to be. You say she's a friend of Austen. Does that mean she still lives in Kansas?"

"Yeah, I know—a long way. But at least I got to spend time with her when I went to help Mark. She was under the impression that Anita and I were serious, so texts and calls had pretty much stopped. I thought she had a special boyfriend too. Which isn't true."

"Oh, I wonder if it was partly my fault regarding Anita," his mother said. "I mentioned once to Austen that you seemed to be spending a lot of time together. Maybe that was my wishful thinking. You know, you're getting older, and I keep hoping someone special will enter your life. So, what are you going to do now?"

"For one thing, I'm going to text and call more to keep me on her mind. Not giving up like I did before."

"So why did you?" she asked.

"Oh, I'm Mr. Macho; sure jumped all over Mark about the way he was acting with Austen," he answered. "Didn't recognize that I was more or less doing the same thing. And I need to make a trip to see her every so often."

Just then he received a text from Mark. "I've got to go. Mark's ready to unload."

As he headed for the door, she asked, "Do you have a picture?"

"No, don't know why I never took one. But just wait 'til you see her beautiful auburn hair."

As he drove toward TrailWays, Josh asked himself why he hadn't at least asked for a picture, or even taken one himself. One can do that with phones now. If he had done that, her picture would always be with him. Maybe Austen would have one; he would check with her as soon as she was home.

He could hold a picture in his hands, kiss her face, trace her lips, touch her hair. Austen might also know the origin of Jerilyn's name. How he loved that name.

When he returned home, first thing he did was call her. Thinking about her was not enough; he needed to hear Jerilyn's voice.

Jerilyn's church group went out to lunch after the services on Sunday. Several were teachers, and the rest were anxious to hear what they did during spring break. She said nothing beyond responding to their reports. So, after they all summed up their recent activities, they turned to her, wanting to know what was happening with Derek.

She responded with, "I'll get to that." She had already shared some of her feelings with the leader and told her about Josh's visit of a few days ago.

After giving a short synopsis of those days in Nebraska, she reminded them also of her return for Austen's wedding and the little that happened during the months in between, up to just a few days ago. Then she told them about her breakup with Derek.

"Even if nothing permanent comes of my feelings for Josh," she told them, "I have no inclination for a relationship with Derek. I'm sure he'll find someone soon who wants to share his life."

One of the others said, "Wow, leave it to quiet Jerilyn to fall into a romantic scenario. Do you have a picture of this western hero? When you get married, will it be here?"

"No, sadly I don't have a picture, wish I did. And there's not going to be a wedding any time soon, if there ever is."

Why had she not taken Josh's picture, or at least asked for one? She was reluctant to ask now that he was back home. Maybe Austen would be able to send her one. She could hold a picture in her hand, touch his face, remember him, remember his kiss, and how he made her feel. All the things Josh had already thought about.

~

Mark had planned to ask Kate to pick up Austen and David, but didn't want to wait. He recalled when they went shopping in Scottsbluff almost a year ago when he could hardly wait for them to return, not yet admitting to himself that he loved her, but hardly able to be apart. Now after this first time of being separated since their marriage, he couldn't bear for it to be any longer. The unloading would have to wait.

Since Mark didn't need his help, Josh drove home and as soon as he entered his house, called Jerilyn. He hoped she wouldn't be busy.

"Hello, Josh." She was still with her friends but rose from her seat and moved to a quieter place.

"Jerilyn."

Her friends couldn't miss the glow that washed across her face as soon as she heard his voice.

"Did you need something?" she asked.

"Yes, I needed to hear your voice. Mark decided to pick up Austen and David himself, so no unloading this afternoon. He and Bill will have to finish up later. Was afraid you might be busy and not able to talk."

"I'm with my church group. We're just finishing lunch," she told him. "And I do need to organize everything for tomorrow's class. Been thinking about presenting facts about the Oregon Trail for a history lesson."

"That's good; maybe it will remind you of me?"

"Maybe."

"I told my mom about you," he said.

"Okay."

"I should have long before," Josh admitted. "Probably would have averted some misunderstanding. Also, talked to Anita." He could almost feel her indrawn breath. "She has never meant any more to me than just a casual friendship, if even that. I know you got a different impression. She tried to imply there was something between us. She has never meant anything to me. She's just a pesky acquaintance."

There was still no more response from her. What else could he say?

"I miss you so much," Josh said, "wish I were heading for the airport to pick you up."

Finally, a word from Jerilyn. "Think I do too."

A few more minutes of conversation, and then a reluctant goodbye from them both. Watching her, the friends chose not to say anything. They could tell that although Jerilyn was happy to hear his voice, ending the call left her sad.

~

On one hand, hearing her voice lifted his spirits, but it reminded Josh of the distance between them. How he wished he could reach out and touch her. Why hadn't he been more assertive when she came for the wedding, when she even stayed in his house? Why did he let his feelings stay covered up when he was attracted to her at first glance? Maybe he could have suggested she transfer to a school in Plattsford. But they hardly knew each other then, and Jerilyn may have looked at that as being too forward. In reality, they still hardly knew each other. How long did it take for that to happen? Did it ever happen? Maybe people married for years never actually knew their mate. Perhaps it was good for there always to be somewhat of a mystery.

No one else had used his spare room since Jerilyn was there. He had hardly been in it himself. Now, perhaps to feel closer to her, he opened the door and walked in. She'd caught the bouquet at the wedding and it still rested on the dresser, the flowers dried, but still with a certain beauty. He picked it up, almost caressingly, then set it down, leaving it for now where she'd placed it.

~

When she got home, Jerilyn took out the notes she'd written after returning from her Oregon Trail trek the previous summer. Some ideas crossed her mind as to how best to use the information for her class. Before school let out for spring break, she piqued their interest by giving them some of the facts. "If you have some time while you're off, maybe you'd like to check it out online."

Subjects or questions she considered assigning to them:

1. Size of wagon—what supplies, food, furniture could they take?
2. What would the students personally want to take?
3. Would the items they named be important to the success of the trip?
4. What would they need to leave behind, and how would they feel about the loss?
5. What would their responsibility be during the trip?

That would probably be enough for the initial lesson. It would depend on how well they did and how much interest they would show as to whether she expanded the lesson.

Maybe Josh would have some ideas that would help the lesson seem more real. As far as she knew, he had lived near the historic trail all his life. But maybe not. That was something she could ask him. She wanted to know as much about him as she could learn. That thought reminded Jerilyn of her plan to ask her dad about the root of her name. Josh wanted to know, and so did she. Why hadn't it occurred to her before she met him?

Her dad answered her text with, "What do you need?"

"I have a question about my name, but I want to see you too. Just checking to see if you're home."

"Nearly always, come on over."

"I usually don't see you as often as I have lately," her dad said as he opened the door for her.

"I know; just feel like I need the connection; maybe I'm missing Josh and wanting to get some answers for him," Jerilyn said. "Don't know why I never questioned it, but he wants to know the origin of my name; and now I do too. I never thought about the fact that I haven't seen it or heard it anywhere else. Though I haven't checked it online either. Maybe it's not as uncommon as I believe."

Jeff asked, "Can I get you coffee, maybe a sandwich?"

"Thanks, no." Then, impulsively, Jerilyn hugged him, with tears in her eyes. "Oh Dad, I have a lost feeling, knowing Josh is so far away. And I can't see there's anything I can do to change it."

Hugging her back, her dad told her, "You're a strong person and I'm sure you'll be able to survive. You'll think of something. It's not like you have to catch a wagon train," he said, grinning. "Now, let's sit at the table; somehow it seems a little more snug and warmer."

She laughed at his mention of a wagon train as she chose a seat.

"You asked about your name. Once upon a time, there were three little girls who were almost inseparable third graders. One was named Marilyn, one Carolyn, and one Joyce. Your mother decided she wanted her name to sound like theirs, so taking her "J", she called herself Jerilyn. The other two, and most of their friends continued to use that name for years. She told everyone, 'If I ever have a little girl, I'm going to name her Jerilyn,' and so she did."

Continuing, he said, "I'm sure there are ladies named Jerilyn, but yours is special; you were named for your mother, even if it is a made-up name."

"Thanks, Dad. I'll try to come visit more often. How are my brothers? Any girlfriends?"

"They're doing okay. If there are any special girls, they haven't shared with me."

"Guess I need to get on home, figure out what I'm going to wear to school tomorrow, and finish my lesson plans. It will be good to have something besides me to occupy my mind. Love you, Dad."

"Love you too."

~

After checking out his extra room, Josh wasn't sure he would want anyone else to stay in it. Not that overnight guests were common for him. If someone needed space, they could stay in his room or sleep on the couch.

School for him wouldn't resume until Tuesday, giving him a full day to prepare lessons—a good thing, since his students had been completely out of his mind for several days, especially the last three.

He thought of Jerilyn's plans to use Oregon Trail information in some upcoming lessons. That was something he occasionally did in the past, even though most of the students practically lived on the trail. Some of their parents even worked for TW—but maybe he could present a different perspective following Jerilyn's format.

Mark texted to let him know they were home, so Josh considered contacting Austen the next day to learn whether she could share any pictures of Jerilyn.

Six

Jerilyn was still much on his mind as Josh climbed into bed, thinking of the bouquet he found on the dresser and recalling the look on her face when she caught it. She had turned to see where he was, held it up, and smiled. What had been on his mind then? What had been on hers?

Finally drifting off to sleep, his dreams were filled with images of her. They were on the trail in the 1840s; Josh was a guide, nearly always on a horse; Jerilyn was travelling with her family, walking most of the time.

It was the end of the day; someone had started a fire and it would be a while before those on foot reached the area where wagons were being circled. She had caught his eye at the beginning, so he checked to see where she was; at the same moment she stepped into a gopher hole and tripped, falling to the ground. Josh immediately rode toward her and was off his horse almost before it stopped, and on his knees to see if she was hurt. This was the closest he had been to her and his heart was pounding. He hoped she was okay, and as Jerilyn turned her face to him, his first thought was how beautiful she was.

Arms reaching out, he planned to help her up, but he too fell, and somehow, they were wrapped in each other's arms. He didn't know she had also been watching him, and realizing how close they were, thought to move, which somehow brought them even closer together. Unaware of all the others who were watching, she raised her hand to his lips as his head lowered to hers, whispering, "Jerilyn—"

He woke, arms around his pillow, and thinking, *What a different perspective.*

~

When she arrived home, instead of getting her lesson materials together, Jerilyn wrote a letter.

> *Dear Josh,*
>
> *I love to hear your voice—and am always glad to get a text, but I'm wanting more than that.*
>
> *I will never regret meeting you—in many ways, I feel you are the half of me that's been missing—a space I haven't been able to fill.*
>
> *And how I wish we could be together more—to touch —to hug —to kiss.*
>
> *There must be some reason that we two somewhat similar souls met—even though we are so many miles and hours apart.*
>
> *So, I am being daring—courageous?—heart in my hand, sending this letter to you—something you can hold, and, I hope, treasure and remember me by.*
>
> *If you're feeling the same way, then I will look forward to receiving a letter from you.*
>
> *Jerilyn*

Realizing she didn't have Josh's address, Jerilyn texted Austen to get it, and at the same time ask her friend if she might have a picture of him she could share. "Don't know why I didn't take a picture myself; guess I wanted to use all the time just being with him."

As soon as she got the address, Jerilyn wrote it on an envelope, folded the letter, inserted it, stamped, and sealed it before she lost her nerve. She would mail it on the way to school the next day.

Austen told her she would get back with her regarding a picture. She was sure she could find one, thinking of the one she took of 'the kiss.' She was contemplating having canvas prints made for both Jerilyn and Josh.

~

It was easy to forget that Josh was in a different time zone than she, making it extra special that he sent a text early that first day back at school.

"Whatever your plans for the day, I pray all goes as you want. Dreamed about you last night. J"

She texted back a simple thanks with a smiling emoji. It was a good start for the day. Jerilyn closed her eyes for a moment, imagining they were together.

Jerilyn checked into classes and learned she could begin evening classes the next week. That was good; being extra busy might help in not missing Josh so much.

~

Austen smiled that morning when she received a text from Josh asking for a picture. Those two—seeming to be behind the times with courtship. But thinking back, they probably didn't expect anything to come from that initial meeting, less than a year ago.

In the middle of the week, Josh's mother called Austen and asked, "Do you have time to talk?"

"Of course."

"Good. Guess I'm being a nosy mother, but a concerned one. And now that I think about it, maybe it would be better if we talked in person. Could you meet me for lunch tomorrow at Eddie's Café? My treat. And you can bring David."

"Austen," Mrs. Wilson greeted her when she entered the café.

"Mrs. Wilson," Austen returned. "David wanted to know if there would be pizza. When I told him probably not, he decided to stay home with Mark."

"Mattie, please. Thank you so much for meeting me. You must be wondering what I want to talk about. I know you're a friend of Jerilyn, this girl Josh is so taken with. I would just like to know a little more about her; and please, don't ever mention this to Josh.

"It's just that he hasn't been in a serious relationship since I can remember, if he ever was," she said. "Sorry to say, I thought Anita O'Neill might be that person and made the mistake of encouraging her. Obviously, she's not the one. But I love him and want him to be happy, and he and Jerilyn are so far apart!"

Austen told her, "Jerilyn is a sweet girl—woman, actually. Did you know she's a teacher too? I've known her for a few years; we met at church and were in the same small group. There hasn't been anyone for her either, but you should have seen them when they met, and more recently when we were together in Kansas." She continued, "Jerilyn told me she wants to have a love like the one Mark and I have. And I believe they have it. I know they'll figure out the best way to take care of the miles apart."

"You know, he apparently doesn't even have a picture of her," Josh's mother said. "I don't know what she looks like, except he told me she has auburn hair."

"And it's beautiful, as she is. You should see the contrast in their coloring. Jerilyn doesn't have a picture of him either; they have both asked me in the last couple of days if I have one of the other that I can share."

Taking out her phone, Austen pulled up some images. "Even in these, you can see the evidence of their feelings for each other, especially 'the kiss.'"

"You're right—no question."

"I'm going to have copies made for them," Austen said.

"Thank you again for meeting me," Mattie said. "Don't know why I was so concerned. And I don't really want to interfere in Josh's life. But maybe you can tell me a bit more about Jerilyn's family?"

"I'm sorry Mrs.—er, Mattie. I think you need to wait until you get that information from your son."

"Yes, you're right. I hope it won't be long."

~

When she got ready to send the text, Jerilyn wondered if Josh had received her letter. How long did it take for mail to be delivered between Overland Park, Kansas, and the Nebraska Panhandle? At any rate, she wasn't going to mention it; she would wait for him to respond.

"Hi, Josh," she texted, "How have your days back at school been? Things good for me. Have learned I can start evening classes next week—will be on Thursday nights from seven to ten. I think of you always. Hugs, Jerilyn."

He called as soon as he got the text.

"Hi, wanted to hear your voice," Josh told her. "School days have been good. And even though my kids pretty much live on the trail, I'm getting some lesson plans together which might present a different viewpoint."

"I asked Austen if she had any pictures of you that she could share," Jerilyn told him.

"And I asked if she had some of you," he replied with a smile in his voice. "How is it we haven't taken any pictures?"

"Probably because we didn't want to interrupt the time we were together."

He asked her, "How's your dad?"

"He's good. I told him I was going to try to visit him more often. Afraid I haven't spent as much time with him as I should, maybe because my brothers are there to be company for him. How's your mother?"

"Good, too. I'll be glad when you two can meet. Soup's warm, so I've got to go. Take care of yourself, and know I'm sending hugs and kisses."

"Bye, same to you."

When would the two ladies be able to meet? And when would he see Jerilyn again? There were no more long breaks scheduled from school. He would check to determine if there might be some days he could take off anyway. Except, if either drove, most of the time would be spent on the road. Maybe it would be easier for Jerilyn to take off, but he couldn't ask her to drive. Perhaps she could fly and stay with him again. Would that be a good idea since their relationship had become so much closer? It was only a few weeks before the end of school, but so many days not being able to see her, and each day seeming longer than the one before. Plus, Josh didn't want to just see Jerilyn; he wanted to hold her in his arms and have another of those kisses like the last one—or was it the first one, or the only one?

He sent a text asking her, "Are there any long weekends or extra days off on your school calendar? Just anxious to know when we can see each other again. One of us would probably have to fly; takes too long to drive for just a couple of days. Hugs."

Jerilyn answered. "I'm sorry, there aren't. And my taking classes makes the possibility even more limited. Hugs back."

At the end of the week, Josh's mother called to see if he could come by after church on Sunday, maybe come for lunch. He wondered what was on her mind; hoped it wasn't to encourage him to spend time with Anita. She seemed to be of the mind recently that he needed someone to spend his life with, and apparently he wasn't able to find that someone by himself. He hoped that she realized Jerilyn was that person; it was just a bit complicated at the time because they were so far apart.

He had received her letter and already read it several times. Jerilyn was right; holding it in his hands helped Josh feel closer to her. And when he missed her most, he could take it out, hold it, and read it again. They were the perfect words. Would he be able to reply in words that were as meaningful?

Seven

Josh saw Anita at church, and when he stopped by his mother's afterward, hoped she wouldn't be there. If so, he would invent some reason for leaving, even though lunch would be good.

At least there was no other car parked in the driveway. Hopefully, that was a good sign. Josh knocked, then walked on in. His mother was busy in the kitchen, gathering things to make lunch. He looked around to be sure Anita wasn't there. She could have ridden with his mother, though unlikely.

"So, is it just you and me?" he asked.

"Who else would it be, unless Nancy was in town?"

"Just wondering. Why do you want to see me?"

"I'm being a nosy mother, but I hope a caring, loving one. Since she is so important to you, I'd like to know more about Jerilyn and her family. And I'm guessing that you're not going to be able to be together for a while; how are you handling that? Etcetera, etcetera."

Ignoring her question, he asked one of his own. "Speaking of Nancy, how's she doing? I haven't been in touch for a while."

"She's fine. I told her about Jerilyn, at least as much as I know about her. I hope that's okay?"

"It's okay," he told her. "I'm hoping, praying, expecting we'll all be family one of these days. And you're certainly correct in guessing that will be a while—at least 'til school's out."

His mother responded with, "But that's only a few months, not really long at all."

"I know," he agreed, almost forlornly, "but it seems like a long time; especially since we're so far apart and there's no way that's going to change for now. We do call and text often but being able to touch would be good."

Mattie thought it certainly sounded like Jerilyn was her son's someone special. And though distance was an obstacle to be overcome, she knew in a few months, things could be much different. Probably one or the other would move, though it would be an interruption in their careers, but if they wanted to be together, that could be worked out.

"I'm glad you've found the woman you want to spend your life with. You no doubt know I was beginning to wonder," she said with a mother's love in her voice. "Can you share anything about her family?"

"Honestly, I can't say I know a lot about them," Josh admitted. "I've been too focused on learning more about her. Her mother died a few years ago, but I met her dad; I like him, and think he likes me. She has two brothers, both younger. One just finished firefighter training, and the other is about ready to graduate from the police academy. They weren't there when I stopped by to see her dad. Not sure what kind of work he did or does. Guess I've just assumed he's retired.

"You know she and Austen Thomas have been good friends for several years. I'm sorry I don't have any pictures to share, but I did ask Austen. I hope she'll have one for me soon. I know what Jerilyn looks like; but I want a picture I can hold."

"I look forward to meeting her and hope it won't be too long," his mother said. "I love you, son."

"Love you too, Mom."

"Okay, it's time to eat. Thank you, God, for this food you have provided, and give Josh and Jerilyn solace as they wait for the time they can be together. Amen."

Jerilyn's brother Jon continued to think about Linda, but still didn't have a phone number. Checking with her parents would be a last resort. He saw in the church bulletin that the Young Singles Group was planning a board-game night. He didn't know whether she would attend, but since he happened to be off, he went.

Everyone was still waiting for the games to start when he walked into the room. He saw Linda immediately. She was standing with a group of young ladies, and he walked up to them, saying, "Hi, I'm Jon," with a special smile for her, continuing with, "Hello, Linda, remember me?"

She blushed, although being a flight attendant, she should have been accustomed to all sorts of flirty approaches. She wasn't sure why Jon's greeting seemed so different. Though he was a brother of her sister's best friend, and they were members of the same church, their age difference meant they were in separate circles of friends. She had only met him twice before—at least recently —and one of those was when she was with her parents. That difference in age could be the reason there was not an earlier connection.

"Of course, I remember you; how could I not?" Turning to the others, she explained, "Jon is Jerilyn Tate's brother. I believe most of you know her. He's a firefighter." Why did she add that? Did it make any difference to anything?

All of them were already curious when he stopped where they were gathered, but as often happens, thinking of him as a hero in uniform made him even more attractive.

As she named each of her friends, he gave a handshake and his cute smile; then he returned to stand close to her. By then, several young males had joined them, each seeming to choose one of the ladies as their game partner for the evening. Jon watched closely, and was glad to see that none of them selected Linda.

He said to her, "You know I don't usually come to these gatherings. Are you willing to be my partner and tutor me in what to expect?"

Later he recalled what a great evening it was, though it might have been mostly because of Linda. They each came in their own car, so they went home separately, but now at least her number was in his phone.

~

It had been a while since Jerilyn sent the letter to Josh. There were phone calls and texts in between, but no mention of the letter. Was it delivered? She didn't want to ask. If he didn't have it, how could she explain why she even wrote it?

In her latest text to him, she reported on the class she was taking. "It's going okay; kind of hard to get back into the habit of studying at the same time I am teaching. And I don't even want to think about upcoming tests. Still unsure as to whether I will want to use it, but I believe it will be a positive thing anyway. Don't remember whether I told you the story about my name. Will explain that in a phone call. Take care. Hugs."

~

He always looked forward to their phone conversations, mainly just because he loved hearing her voice. He wasn't even sure how much attention he paid to what she was telling him. Now he thought, *I've waited long enough to reply to her letter. She hasn't mentioned the one she sent, so she's probably wondering.*

Dear Jerilyn,

Dearest Jerilyn, how I love that name; how I love saying it. It's almost poetic.

I love your letter. I love holding it in my hand and reading it over and over. I'm glad you were daring enough to write it, to send it.

I will keep it forever. It expresses so well the way I feel. And for now it seems we still have to remain apart. I pray it will be a short time.

I long for the time we aren't; the time when all we need to be able to touch, to kiss, to hug, is to reach out and wrap our arms around each other.

Hugs and kisses,
Josh

Just as Jerilyn didn't mention the letter she sent, neither would he. It could be like a romantic game between them. An expectancy, an anticipation between their delivery; no idea of when that would be. Perhaps it would work toward making the months, the weeks, the days pass more quickly.

Josh wrote her name on an envelope and checked the return label on the one she sent to be sure he got the address correct. Then just as she did, he folded the letter, inserted it, stamped the envelope then sealed it. Holding it up, he was tempted to seal it with a kiss, then thought, why not. *When you receive this, Jerilyn, I hope you sense the kiss that I wish I could give you.*

The same day Josh's letter went out in the mail, Austen sent some pictures to Jerilyn. In addition to copies of some snapshots, there was the canvas print of 'the kiss' as she called it. Both Jerilyn and Josh would get one. She wasn't sure yet how to get Josh's to him, but would try to gauge when Jerilyn would receive hers, so he would get his close to the same time.

They hadn't talked for a while and Jerilyn was anxious to hear his voice, so called Josh a few nights later. There was no specific reason, except she still needed to tell him the origin of her name. "I like that story," he told her. "Of course, you know I like your name, however you got it. And I don't believe I've ever heard you say what your dad's career is, or was?"

"I'm sure it hasn't been mentioned. He's a retired Police Lieutenant. Now he keeps busy volunteering at various historical venues.

"And no more news," she told him. "I just mostly wanted to hear your voice. Have some school papers I need to grade, and probably need to study for my class too. Take care."

"You too; bye."

~

Jerilyn received the letter from Josh as well as the pictures from Austen after a challenging day at school, so they were special gifts. She debated which to open first and settled on the pictures. She wanted to have his image in front of her when she read his letter. There were snapshots of him on his horse as the Pony Express Rider, and a couple taken with Mark. She saved for last the large one which was wrapped carefully in tissue paper.

She was shocked when it was completely revealed. It was a canvas print, and the couple stood kissing with arms wrapped around each other; his blonde hair and her auburn left no question that it was her and Josh.

A knot formed in her stomach as she stared at it and the memory of that day rushed over her. There had been no awareness of anyone except themselves as the kiss transpired. Apparently even Austen knew it was special as she snapped it. It was strange knowing this was their first kiss, and so far, the last. Would there ever be others, and when?

She held it, staring at it, pressing it against her heart with tears in her eyes.

"Oh, Josh. I miss you so much."

Finally, she set it aside, close by so she could see it as she read his letter.

~

Austen debated as to how and when to get pictures to Josh. Mark suggested they invite him for a meal; it was getting close to time for planning TrailWays' summer session, and they could discuss it. He remembered Josh's mentioning taking classes, which might mean he couldn't help this year.

They settled for Sunday after church and texted to ask whether he was available.

"Sure am. I'm a so-so cook; always open to letting someone else provide a meal."

During their discussion of TrailWays' upcoming season, Mark said to Josh, "You've been an important part of TW for several years. Will that still be true this coming summer?"

Josh answered with, "I mentioned to you that I may take classes this summer, and don't know yet how much time that would take. But I'd like to continue, maybe part-time if it would work for you."

"What about time with Jerilyn?" Mark asked.

"Yeah, there's that—and actually the most important—just don't want to let you down."

"You couldn't do that," Mark told him. "Your being around in the early years made a big difference in our success. And whatever—any time you can help is always appreciated. You did tell me you were thinking of taking classes, but don't remember whether you gave a reason."

Josh answered, "I've got it in my mind I might want to become a principal, and I'm fairly sure there are certain classes I need to accomplish that. If I'm looking to be a married man, thought that would be a positive thing."

"Oh yeah, now I remember. We'll sure pray for the best for you and Jerilyn."

Austen handed Josh a package and told him, "This is one of the reasons we asked you over."

She crossed her fingers, hoping Jerilyn had not yet mentioned the pictures, not sure why it made a difference to her. And Jerilyn hadn't. It was almost a habit for one of them to call on Sunday nights when there was more time for sharing. So as yet there had been no telling.

Opening the package Austen had handed to him, he saw a few snapshots of Jerilyn—one of her alone, and others with her church friends. He took a bit of time, looking at each one, quietly tracing her face with his finger. David wanted to see the pictures, so Josh lifted him onto his lap.

David remembered seeing her those several weeks ago. "That's Jer'lin. She lives in Kansas."

"Yes, she does, a long way from here."

David noticed tears, touched Josh's face, and asked, "Why are you crying?"

"Because I miss her."

Then he unwrapped the canvas print. Seeing the heart-breaking look on his face, Mark and Austen rose and began quietly clearing the table. Taking David's hand, Mark led him away and turned to a program on TV that would occupy his mind.

Giving him some time to absorb the scene in the picture, Austen told him, "I'm sorry, I thought you would want this picture specially to remind you of her."

"Oh, it's wonderful; and thank you for all of them. Maybe you sent a copy to her?"

"I did. Just couldn't help taking the picture when I saw you two. I hope you don't feel it was an invasion of privacy? You were so wrapped up in each other, and so overflowing with love, I wanted to capture it. Jerilyn has told me she wants a love like mine and Mark's; and I think she has it with you."

"I hope so."

"I haven't heard from her since I sent the pictures, so not sure how she feels about it," Austen told him.

"Despite my initial reaction, I'm glad you took the picture. Don't know if I will show it to my mother," Josh said. "The others will do to let her see one reason I love Jerilyn."

Austen chose not to tell him about showing his mother the pictures on her phone.

"We often talk on Sundays. I'll call her later; see what she thinks of it," Josh said.

He called Jerilyn as soon as he got home.

She was looking at the picture when she answered, "Josh, hi."

"Just came from lunch with Mark and Austen," he told her. "She gave me some pictures you're in, then that special one of our kiss. She said she sent one to you too?"

"Yes. Quite a surprise. I'm glad to have it. Makes me happy and sad at the same time. Sad you're not here, but happy remembering that kiss and how it felt, how I felt. Makes me feel closer to you, but still with a longing to touch you, to feel your arms around me."

"I pretty much feel the same way. I'll show Mom the other pictures Austen gave me, but this one's going to stay in my room where I'll be the only one who sees it."

"Strange how life is sometimes," Jerilyn said. "Mark and Austen were together every day, though often in contention. We've longed to have a reminder so we can see each other every day."

"Yeah," he agreed, then asked, "How are your classes going?"

"Which one?"

"Both."

"Think I'm finally learning how to study again—maybe that will help with my students," Jerilyn opined. "And they're doing well—the Oregon Trail lessons were a success. Some of them want to experience the trail at TrailWays sometime. You?"

Josh replied, "School kids doing okay. I know more now about possible summer classes for me. Regarding that, I want to suggest something to you. If I take classes, it won't leave much free time for me. Could you, would you consider coming to Plattsford for a couple of weeks this summer? Don't say anything now; just think about it and we'll talk more later. I so much need to see you and hold you."

"Okay."

"Talk to you later. Bye."

"Bye."

Eight

After talking to Josh, rereading his letter, and poring over the pictures again, Jerilyn wrote another letter to him.

Dear Josh,

Your letter meant so much to me. The pictures Austen sent came the same day. I kept them in front of me as I read it. And I will probably do so each time I take it out to read again.

When I look at the calendar, I am surprised at how much time has passed since we were together, but, oh, how much time stretches in front of us. I hope it will be a bit easier since I have pictures of you.

I will consider a possible trip this summer. If I come, where will I stay?

You are always on my mind and in my heart.

Jerilyn

Except for occasionally passing in the hallway at school, Jerilyn had not seen Derek since she left him at Cinzetti's. Now on this teachers' workday, she saw him coming toward the table where she was sitting. She had arrived early and was alone.

Taking a seat across from her, Derek greeted her with, "Hello, Jer, what have you been doing these last few weeks?"

"My name is Jerilyn," she told him.

Obviously puzzled, he responded, "Huh? Yeah, I know that."

"Then don't call me Jer."

"Okay—so anything interesting in your life?" he asked. "Any plans for the summer?"

"You may have heard I'm taking classes." She wasn't going to bother telling him what the classes were for. "And so far, no definite plans for summer, though there is something pending."

Ignoring her statement, he told her, "I'm thinking about going on a cruise, just not sure where yet."

"That's nice," she said, though she wondered why he was mentioning it.

He continued, ignoring her obvious disinterest. "Really need to find someone to go with me. Any ideas as to anyone I can ask?"

She was thinking, *How did I ever make a decision to go out with him, even as a friend? Must have been because I was missing Josh so much and thinking we would never be together. It's as if he has no intuition of ordinary, acceptable conversation.*

"No, I don't," she told him without any more comment.

Others were filling up the seats, and she was thankful to have her friend Lainie take the one next to her.

Jerilyn wasn't the type to ignore anyone, but she definitely wanted to ignore Derek.

"Hey, Jerilyn, I heard your lessons about the Oregon Trail were quite successful," Lainie told her. "Maybe we can have a combined class next year."

"Maybe." She didn't want to commit more than that; perhaps she would be somewhere else next year.

"Have you talked to Josh lately?" her friend asked.

Smiling, Jerilyn said, "Yes, and texted, and Austen sent some pictures."

"Ooh, can I see?"

Jerilyn replied, "They're all at home. You'll have to stop by to see them sometime."

At Lainie's question about Josh, Derek looked puzzled. Though she'd told him that night at Cinzetti's that there was someone else, he was so wrapped up in himself, he apparently hadn't comprehended how serious she was. And though she may have embellished a bit, the fact remained she didn't want to spend any more time with him.

Still with no idea when not to insert his thoughts into a conversation, Derek asked, "Who's Josh?"

Jerilyn ignored the question, but Lainie answered with a swooning "Don't you know he's her Nebraska love? He was even here over spring break. She kept him to herself and most of us didn't get to see him."

She was purposely laying it on thick, grinning at Jerilyn, who mouthed, "Thank you." She almost felt sorry for him as she noted his puzzlement. He was probably remembering that it was during spring break when he made his odd proposal.

Then the activities started, so there was no more time for conversation.

Jerilyn mailed the letter to Josh on her way to school. She still didn't know how long it took the mail to get to him. But she did look at the calendar to consider dates for a possible visit. Besides having the time with Josh, she knew there would be visits with his mother, and hoped they would like each other.

~

It was amazing how quickly the last few weeks of school were passing—especially after the dreariness of the fall and winter months, when there had been no communication with Jerilyn. Hopefully, that would never happen again. And though Josh would very much like to be able to hold her, at least now there were regular texts, phone calls, and even letters.

He was so glad she initiated that. As Jerilyn had expected, it was fulfilling to hold the letter and reread it—especially with her pictures in front of him. He wondered when he might receive another.

Now that the days and times of his summer class were confirmed, he hoped Jerilyn would decide to come to spend some time with him. But even if she did, the earliest would probably be in five to six weeks. And right now, that seemed like such a long time. It might as well be five to six months. Josh had left the decision to her; so, hard as it was, he would wait to hear from her before mentioning the invitation again.

He should be thinking about what they would do when she came. They couldn't just sit and grin at each other, or hug each other, or kiss each other—well, maybe part of the time.

~

His sister Nancy, who was a physical therapist, lived in Scottsbluff. She was a couple years younger than he and still single. His mother had told her about Jerilyn and knowing he didn't communicate with her nearly enough, Josh decided to call.

"Hello."

"Hi, it's your brother."

"I know; what a surprise; is everything okay?"

"Yeah, I know I'm the worst about keeping in touch," he said.

"Well, to be honest, I know I haven't been any better," Nancy admitted. "We need to change that. So, Mom told me you've found someone special."

"Yeah, Jerilyn. I met her last summer when she came to visit her friend Austen at TrailWays—you know she married Mark Thomas."

"And she's from Kansas?"

"Kind of interesting, don't you think? Mark married someone from Kansas, and I hope to."

"That serious, huh? Don't think you've been interested in anyone since your almost fiancée. Have you mentioned her to your Jerilyn?" Nancy asked.

"I haven't thought about that fiasco forever. And I'm not sure Jerilyn really knows how I feel. Counting time we've been together face-to-face, it only adds up to about a week."

"Wow!" his sister exclaimed. "I can hardly wait to meet her."

"Since I'm taking a class this summer, I've asked if she can come visit for a couple of weeks. Don't have an answer from her yet."

"And your class is for?"

"Since I'm thinking of marriage, I'm considering what I need to become a principal," he told her. "So, the classes would be leading toward that."

"You're just full of surprises."

"Anything new with you?" Josh asked. "Someone special?"

"Nothing new, and no one special. At least not yet."

"Glad I called. Been good talking to you."

"You too; love you, Bro."

"You too. Bye."

"Bye."

~

When he got Jerilyn's letter in the mail, he thought again about Nancy's reminder of Sherise, giving him something else to think about and wondering whether to tell Jerilyn about her. It would probably be better for him to mention it than for her to hear it from someone else. But when would be a good time? There might not be such a thing; no matter when it happened, it wouldn't be easy, and how would she respond?

Dearest Jerilyn,

It's always a wonderful day when I get a letter from you. And the most recent one telling me you will consider a visit this coming summer really lifted my spirits.

You can probably guess that I would prefer—actually love—to have you stay with me? But if that would make you uncomfortable, I can check with my mother. I'm sure she would be happy to have you.

Had a long phone visit with my sister. I told her how special you are. She's anxious to meet you.

Still so many weeks to wait.

Sending hugs and kisses and love,

Josh

~

The women in her church group were curious about Josh—what he looked like, his personality, and whatever else it was that she fell in love with. So Jerilyn invited them to come to her house for the next meeting. They usually met at a restaurant and had a meal, as well as study time.

They ordered sandwiches from Good Cents and she provided coffee, soft drinks, and water.

They began with the study, but most of them were too interested in learning about Josh and seeing his picture to pay much attention, so study time was cut short. They went to the kitchen to get their sandwiches and drinks while she went to her bedroom to get the pictures.

But before she could show them, there was a knock at the door. She was surprised to see her brother, Jack. He would have seen the extra cars, which should have alerted him that she had company.

"Hi, can I come in?" he asked.

She told him, "My group is here."

"I know, I can see the cars."

"So, is that why you're here, to meet girls? Some of them are married, you know."

"Yes, I do," he admitted, "but some aren't."

"They're probably all older than you," Jerilyn told him.

"That's okay, I like older women."

Giving one more questioning look, she said, "You might as well come on in."

Maggie and a couple of the others recognized him. "Hello, Jack."

"Hi, all. For those who may not know me, I'm Jerilyn's brother. Do you think we look alike?"

She led him around the room, naming each woman he didn't know. Then from him, "Oh boy, Good Cents. Do you have enough for me?"

She told him, "Go ahead, help yourself. We finished study early because I was going to tell them about Josh and show them his pictures."

"Oh, I want to know about Josh and see what he looks like."

The exasperated look on her face told him that was as much teasing as he should do for now. Then with his sandwich and a drink in his hand, looked around for a place to sit. The two women on the couch looked at each other, then separated so he could sit between them.

Thanking them, he said to his sister, "Why don't you start with the pictures?"

They were all anxious to know more about Josh, but now there was a new personage they wanted to know more about. Someone asked him what he did, and he told them, "This is about Josh. You can learn about me next time," smiling at his sister as he said it.

She started with the picture of Josh on his horse as the Pony Express Rider. They glanced from the picture to her, as if trying to imagine them together.

"Maggie knows all this, and I've told one or two of you about our first meeting. He had just come in from the trail. The Pearsons asked us to have a meal with them, then invited Josh to join us too. The next day he came by while we were out on a short trek. He asked if I wanted to ride with him back to headquarters." She paused briefly before adding, with a grin, "I did. The other man in this picture is Mark—the owner, and the man that Austen married."

She passed the pictures around, with Jack paying as much attention as the women. The picture of the kiss was the last one in her hand, and she held it a bit longer.

"Austen took this picture just before Mark and Josh climbed into the truck to drive back to Nebraska. I knew nothing about it until she sent it to me."

She handed it to Jack first who studied it closely, looking at his sister who had a heartrending look on her face. He passed it on, then stood to give Jerilyn a hug.

"I love you, Sis." Turning to the others, he said, "Ladies, thank you for letting me join you. I need to go now. See you at church? Bye."

Despite all that was happening, she noticed a couple of her friends taking extra note of him as he went out the door. Then as they finished looking at the pictures, they wanted a few more details about Josh and what was happening in their lives.

After watching the group while Jack was with them, it was no surprise to her that her friends wanted to know more about him.

"He's about ready to graduate from the Police Academy."

"Ooh. Bet he really looks hot in his uniform."

Jerilyn noticed that one of the girls, usually shy, was blushing. She was also one of those who gave him some special attention.

"He's probably younger than most of you."

From a couple of them: "That's no problem."

As soon as all the girls were gone, she texted her brother.

"Was good to see you, but why?"

"Not sure," he told her. "I felt an overwhelming urge to come by. Didn't know 'til I got there that your group was meeting. Good to meet them all."

"They liked you too. I think especially Jayden and Merritt."

"Can't tell you I remember specifically," he said, "but I think, me too."

Jerilyn said, "Thought you had a girlfriend."

"Naw, that didn't work out."

Nine

It was unusual on the next Sunday that all four Tates went to church together. But as they entered the worship center, some of the ladies in Jerilyn's group were sitting together and motioned for Jack to join them. The other three Tates smiled and nodded their heads for him to go.

Then Jon spied Linda and wasted no time strolling to where she was. He tapped her on the shoulder, and she turned, giving a smile, and moved so he could join her. He noticed earlier in the week that their band was performing at a venue in KC and asked her to go, so there was something special to look forward to.

Jerilyn and her dad looked at each other, and said, "Looks like it's just the two of us as usual."

After church, she sent a text to Josh. "The beginning of a new week, and we Tates went to church together. But Jack joined a couple of my friends. Then Jon sat with Linda—Austen's sister. So it was Dad and me again. We are planning lunch together.

"I'm jealous they can be with people that might become special to them when you and I are so far apart. I hope that won't be true much longer. Days and weeks are passing, though not quickly enough. Hugs."

As soon as he received the text, he called.

"Hi, Josh."

"Jerilyn. Texts are great, but I needed to hear your voice. Wish we could have been together in church this morning. I did go with my mother. Does Austen know her sister and your brother are becoming an item?"

"Don't know," she told him. "I haven't said anything to her; for now, I'm leaving it to Linda. It is a new relationship. Do you have a starting date for your classes?"

"Should know tomorrow," he told her. "But it will be around the first of June."

"That's still a few weeks," Jerilyn said.

"Yeah, excited and dreading it at the same time," he admitted. "Wish you were here to hold my hand and give me encouragement."

"I'm sure you'll do fine, but I've learned school is a bit different when one is older."

"So, when will you be finished with your class?" Josh asked.

"End of May or first part of June."

"We can compare later. Supposed to go to Mom's, so have to sign off.

Love you."

"You too, bye."

Why was she beginning to feel that despite the letters, texts, and calls, their separation seemed to be getting wider? They even decided when her trip to Nebraska would be—the last week in June and first week of July. But that was still weeks away. There were her classes; his hadn't started yet.

Maybe she would call Austen. They texted regularly, but it would be good to talk to her. Plus, she might get a hint regarding Josh; she felt there was something he was holding back. How could she be filled with love the same time she was filled with dread, or was it just uncertainty?

At least the days were getting longer and there was more sunshine. Maybe that's all it was—seasonal affective disorder. She needed to set aside this melancholy and have only happy thoughts.

~

When her brothers arrived for lunch, she thought how rare these gatherings were. First, they had gone to church together, and now a meal with all of them. Of course, as it happened, they didn't sit together at church since her brothers ended up sitting with the girls they recently met.

Watching her father, she could tell it meant a lot to him. How would he be affected if she moved away? Why hadn't she thought of that before?

But she could almost hear him say, "You have to live your life for you—not for me."

Happy thoughts, Jerilyn, happy thoughts.

Since they were rarely able to have lunch together, there was much to talk about. Her brothers related some of their experiences in their training, with no mention of the dangers associated with the careers they had chosen. So far, thankfully, there had been none for them.

Since watching them in church that morning, Jeff asked his sons about the women they sat with.

"Not that it bothers me, but you both are getting along in age," laughing as he said it.

Jerilyn knew just a bit more, but she wondered too, especially where Jack was concerned.

Jon spoke up first. "Well—you know Linda Morgan is Austen's sister. But I never paid any attention to her—she's younger, you know—until some weeks ago. Even then, I didn't get a phone number until I realized she was on my mind a lot. Lately we've been at some of the same places and events; no actual dates yet."

Noticing a look from his sister, he added, "Except we are going to hear Ron's Band in a few days."

Then Jeff turned to Jack with a question on his face.

Who told them, "I don't even know as much as Jon. I met them at Jerilyn's group and heard everyone's names, but I don't even know for sure the names of those I sat with."

That wasn't the whole truth. He did recognize Jayden, though he didn't know her full name, nor the name of the other woman.

He glanced at Jerilyn, who told him, "The blonde was Merritt Long, and the other, Jayden Black."

"I'll try to remember. Bad thing is, not acquainted with them well enough to know which I like best. And how can one come between friends?"

He did already know he liked Jayden but couldn't say he knew her. He had only noticed her at church occasionally, but those glances had fascinated him. He wanted to learn more about her.

Jerilyn told him, "I can help you there. Merritt is dating, seriously, I think. So that leaves Jayden—goodness, another 'J.' But knowing her and knowing you, you're complete opposites. Not sure she's even dated much. But I know enough to tell you she's particular."

Undaunted, Jack said, "Maybe you can give me her phone number?"

"Not yet, but I do know she enjoys Ron's Band too and sometimes goes with some of the other girls in the group. Maybe you can show up at his next gig? Seems like Jon and Linda will be there."

He was disappointed but accepted what she told him.

Throughout these conversations, she was thinking, *How strange life sometimes is. Suddenly, my brothers are interested in women who are somehow connected with me. I think I like it.*

Jeff told them, "Well it all sounds good to me. Hope you boys will keep me informed." Then he turned to his daughter, who simply shook her head.

~

Before she started her class, Jerilyn learned she had already met most of the requirements to be a special ed teacher. Taking the class could still be a positive thing, but if she should end up in Nebraska, she wasn't sure whether it would be used.

And would a possible transfer to a Nebraska school occur before the school term started in September? Or would she still be in Kansas, where there always seemed to be openings for teachers somewhere, but especially those in special ed? Maybe she would still be in the same school, with the same grade.

Jerilyn did know that one moving to another state and hoping for a position would need to file paperwork and pay a fee to get a license for teaching there. How long might that take? How soon would she know whether to start that process?

It was difficult to not be anxious regarding her unknown future. Would that be settled after her visit? Seemed to her it would be much more complicated if she continued in her present classroom in Kansas and then moved. And would there be a position for her in Nebraska, specifically Plattsford, if school were already in session? If not, then what would she do? Then she reminded herself again to keep from worrying. *Happy thoughts, happy thoughts.*

As she pondered what the summer might bring, Jerilyn reminded herself that Austen and Mark had taken three months of summer to make a loving commitment, and that at almost the last minute.

Should she make the first move toward making Josh's and her relationship permanent? She didn't want to; she wanted Josh to be the one. Besides, she had no clue what she would do to initiate the process.

Maybe she should ask him what he knew about the chance of getting a position in Plattsford or nearby schools. And what about him? Was he thinking there would be an opening for a principal before the beginning of school? And when was that? If she wasn't going to be with him soon, she didn't want to move. Well, no decision needed to be made yet. She would wait until after her visit.

Dear Josh,

I'm looking forward to those two weeks when I will be with you. Guess we could say "almost soon." Sorry to tell you that at the same time I'm already worried—concerned about what will happen in the fall. You—we—haven't talked about that at all.

I will try to set that aside. I want our letters to be positive—loving—no questions—no worries. I want to be with you—no more separations. It will be hard enough when I leave after the summer visit. And though it's not that many weeks until that time, it won't be easy.

With my love, Jerilyn

Needing something to lessen her concerns, she called Austen. Though they kept in touch regularly with texts, she hoped there might be some reassurance from someone who had experienced a similar problem less than a year before.

"Hello, Jerilyn. This is a surprise. What's going on?"

"I don't know," Jerilyn told her. "Maybe I just need to talk to someone who sees and talks to Josh occasionally. Don't know why, but I feel every day we're farther apart. And yes, we text and phone and there are even letters, but I want something more."

"Aren't you coming to visit soon?"

"I am, but look at the calendar. That's still weeks away."

"My goodness, how did you make it through those weeks between November and when we were there in March?" Austen asked.

"Not very well, but I had given up hope of ever being with him then."

"I'm sorry," Austen told her. "At least Mark was always with me, though we weren't getting along very well. We do see Josh occasionally, and I think he's probably feeling the same as you. Maybe it would help if you called more often, even if you always have to be the one to do it? And maybe I can discreetly ask questions? Actually, no," she said, "I think I'll mention this conversation to Mark. If you remember, it was Josh who pushed Mark. Maybe Mark needs to push Josh?"

"Oh, that sounds good. I'm so glad I called," Jerilyn said. "So how are you feeling? Is your pregnancy going okay?"

After a little more conversation, they said goodbye.

Ten

Mark laughed when Austen told him about Jerilyn's feelings, thinking of how Josh jumped all over him last summer regarding his relationship with Austen.

With that on his mind, Mark went to his wife, wrapping her in his arms and saying, "I'm so sorry it took me so long to come to my senses. Don't know what Josh is thinking, guess he doesn't remember. I'll see if I can take him to lunch and try to talk some sense into him. He's probably thinking only from his viewpoint and not considering Jerilyn at all. Unfortunately, we men are like that sometimes," he told her as he grinned.

~

The men met for lunch in Plattsford and spent some time discussing TrailWays and what might be happening when the season started.

Mark laughed and said, "That hand I hired last year isn't available. So I need to get someone else. And maybe for your position too? I recall that Austen told me about some young girls on one of the treks who became quite interested in the operation. Maybe I need to consider a change that would include some younger people—even females.

"So, Josh, you still planning to take classes this summer?"

"Well, yes. Remember I told you I was thinking to find out what's required of a school principal—classes, degrees, etc. if I were going to get married."

"What does Jerilyn think of that?" Mark asked him. "Have you mentioned the 'why,' especially since it would keep you here? No time to go visit her and move forward in your relationship, even if she has seemed to react positively?"

Josh looked confused and questioning, indicating that thought had never crossed his mind.

Mark continued, "You know that can always happen later, after you're married. And when do you think a wedding would take place, and where? Apparently in your mind it's a done thing. Have there been any conversations between you and Jerilyn about it?

"If you remember, Austen and I were at least together, even though, unfortunately, we were in constant contention. Don't believe Jerilyn can gauge your feelings from Kansas."

"We talk and text, and even write letters," Josh replied.

"But you can't touch, or at least be close together," Mark reminded him. "I remember that trip from Kansas, when you were talking as if there was nothing that could change your being apart and how it was affecting you. I'm not sure you're making the right plans. Maybe you should go see her. There's a long weekend coming up. And one more thing; maybe you need to tell her about Sherise."

That surprised Josh; first Nancy, and now Mark. And there were probably others who might bring up the subject. Remembering how Tricia showed up before Mark mentioned her to Austen, he knew it was probably good advice.

~

A couple of days after his conversation with Mark, Josh received Jerilyn's latest letter. Reading it, he almost felt her anguish and thought the other man was certainly right. Why did he have to remind himself he hadn't specifically asked her about marriage? Would it be fair to ask her when he still felt uncertain about what he might be doing?

~

After her phone call with Austen, Jerilyn decided to call her dad. Maybe he could give her some advice; or at least she could get his view on her problem if that's what it was.

"Hey, Dad, would you like to have supper with me sometime?"

"What's the occasion?" he asked.

"Kind of complicated—too much to try to explain on the phone. I'll even cook."

"You've got my curiosity up. So, you have a day in mind?"

"How about Saturday, five thirty?"

"I'll be there," he told her. "Are you inviting your brothers?"

"No, this time, just you and me."

~

When Saturday came, she greeted her dad with a smile. "So glad you came," then began to cry.

"Oh, Jerilyn, what's wrong?"

"Probably nothing, but I'm feeling so confused and lost in my relationship with Josh. Maybe I'm expecting too much."

They moved further into the house as she continued, "That's why I invited you, to ask you about you and Mom. I know you didn't have a long-distance courtship, but how did things go? When did you know you wanted to be together? Then how long before you proposed?" Smiling, she asked, "Maybe Mom did?"

He laughed at that, and said, "No, but I think she was ready to. And I would have accepted."

"I asked you here for a meal, so let's go on into the kitchen. You can tell me the rest of the story after we eat."

Her dad began with when he and her mother had met. "They didn't have Meet and Greet events then, but it was similar. I gave her my card, so she was first to call. Then I made sure I got her phone number and address.

"You asked when we knew we wanted to be together. I think I can honestly say immediately, or at least by the end of our first date. And if you ask me, I think that's true of most happily married couples. It just takes a while for some to admit it. As you said, it wasn't long distance, but we called each other, and I went by her house as often as I could. Think it irritated your grandparents, especially when I was in my patrol car."

Continuing, he said, "And I was only a patrolman, didn't think I was earning enough to support a wife. You asked if your mom proposed. She didn't actually, but she pointed out that there would be two paychecks, at least at the beginning. And we might not be able to live lavishly, but that wasn't us anyway. We both pretty much liked more simple things, but we loved each other.

"You probably know the rest. I proposed, asked your grandfather for her hand, and six months after our meeting, we got married. We didn't want to be apart. So, are you thinking of proposing?"

"Yeah, maybe," she told him.

~

Josh couldn't stop thinking about his conversation with Mark. And it all made sense. Why had he thought he needed to change his life before considering marriage? Instead, he should have tried to figure out how often he could visit Jerilyn. Yes, she would be coming to visit him, but even then, he would be gone part of the time, especially if he continued with his plan to attend classes.

He should call or text her, but with those new things to consider, he was feeling uncertain about what he might say. And he wanted to write a letter, but what would he write? It had been too many days since being in touch with her.

He looked at the pile of classwork from his students waiting to be graded. But for now, he chose to just close his eyes, then sit and think for a while.

~

Finally deciding to talk to her, he called Jerilyn.

"Who is this?"

"Josh."

"Who?"

"Josh."

"Do I know you?"

"Come on, Jerilyn, it hasn't been that long since we've been in touch."

"How do you know my name?"

By then, his heart was beating rapidly; he didn't like the teasing.

"Okay, this isn't funny anymore. I'm sorry if you think I've been tardy with my texts, calls, and letters."

"Letters?"

"Yes, I owe you one."

"Sorry, I don't know who you are," then she hung up.

How did that happen? Didn't she know how important she was to him? How had he not conveyed his love?

He would call Austen, ask her about Jerilyn.

The phone rang, waking him up. It was his mother.

"Oh, Mom, thank you so much for calling."

~

Memorial Day wasn't that much earlier than the date Jerilyn would be visiting, but he would have four days more or less free. Instead of checking with her, he got Jeff Tate's phone number from Austen and called him.

"This is Josh Wilson."

"I can see that."

"Don't want to burden you with my problems, or one might say fears. I'm feeling Jerilyn is becoming apprehensive concerning our relationship or is already. So, I'm calling for advice."

"Not sure I can help you," Jeff replied.

"I'm just wondering if she may have plans for the weekend of Memorial Day. I'm free on those days, and I want to see her."

"Okay."

Josh asked, "How do you think she would react to my just showing up? I could fly in and rent a car."

Remembering his recent supper with her, Jeff said, "Now that you mention it, she has been kind of mopey lately—maybe partly because her brothers seem to have found their special ladies. Don't know if she has plans, but I can probably think of a way to be sure she's in town. Why don't you just come here? You can even stay with me if you need to. Text me the times. And before you ask, yes, I do text."

"That's great. Thank you so much, Mr. Tate."

"Jeff."

"Okay, Jeff, I'll get back to you."

~

"Josh."

"Hello, Jerilyn. I've missed hearing your voice, seems like forever."

"Yes, me too."

"I had a dream, actually a nightmare. I called you and you didn't know who I was. Are you crying?"

"Yes, I'm so sorry," she said. "I hurt thinking of how you must have felt. No matter what happens, I will always know you."

"I hope you plan to stay with me when you come to Plattsford. Being together should help us get to know each other, and maybe love each other more. And I do love you," he told her.

"I love you too."

"Wish I could hold you right now. Let's think about changing things so we can always be together—soon."

"I'm for that," she agreed.

Josh told her, "Glad I got to share these thoughts. Should have long ago."

"I'm glad too."

"Let's talk again soon."

Jerilyn told him, "I'll call next time. Love you."

"You, too."

~

Realizing he may not have kept in touch with her as often as he should have, Josh wrote a letter as soon as he hung up.

Dearest Jerilyn,

I felt like I was lost somewhere before our phone visit. It's still too long before you come. I'm asking myself, why didn't I plan differently?

Have decided I'm a dodo. I need your influence to make me think more clearly.

See you soon, but not soon enough. I don't want you to not know me.

All my love,
Josh

~

It was hard for him to stay mum about his plans to see her soon when he called and sent texts, which were now daily for one or the other. He didn't intend for there to be any possibility for a time when she wouldn't know him.

And he learned, though he should have already known, that his efforts helped him feel closer to her. Why had he become lax in keeping in touch? Was he perhaps thinking more about a possible future than the appreciation of the present? For him, it was still a journey for love; and for now, that journey would be to Kansas again.

~

Jeff received a text from Josh with his plans. "The available flights and my schedule don't allow me to go before Saturday morning, probably arriving at your place about ten o'clock, and leaving Monday afternoon. Hope I will be able to stay with Jerilyn. I do need your address and thank you so much."

~

"Hello, Mom."

"Josh, you okay? You sound distracted."

"I may be. Lots of stuff swirling around in my head," he told her.

"Like?"

"Too complicated to try to explain. But I'm glad you called. Need to tell you I'm going to visit Jerilyn Memorial Day weekend."

"But won't she be here right after that?" his mother asked.

"Yes," he said, "but this is important. I'm going to surprise her."

"What if she's not there?" Mattie asked.

"She will be. Her dad's making sure."

"That's a long way. Are you driving?"

"No, going to fly. And, Mom, I need your prayers."

"Always. Anything else?"

"No, sorry I don't call you more, or even stop by. How about I take you out to eat tonight?"

Eleven

Jeff called Jerilyn to ask if she could come to his house Saturday morning. He was glad she didn't inquire why, because he could think of no good reason. He did tell her that her brothers would probably be there too.

"Any particular time?"

"Ten would be good."

The boys knew that Josh was expected and intended to confront him about his relationship with their sister and ask about his intentions. They would wear their uniforms, though neither would be on duty until later in the day.

~

Josh was on the plane and wanting to take off, with no more delays keeping him from Jerilyn. What would she think when she saw him? Would it be awkward? He hoped not; he could see himself wrapping his arms around her, holding her, and not wanting to let go. He had asked his mother to pray, and he too prayed for a safe trip and a sweet reunion with Jerilyn.

When they were in the air, the man in the next seat asked, "Going to Kansas City?"

"Yeah," Josh told him.

"Been there before?" the man asked.

"Once; you?"

"Actually, I'm going to Overland Park to visit some cousins."

"That's where I'm headed—to see my girlfriend. She doesn't know I'm coming."

Girlfriend. He had never said that before, and truthfully had never thought of her as his girlfriend. Jerilyn was so much more than that; she filled an empty space in him. He was not, could not, be whole without her.

The man asked, "Is that a good idea? She might not be home."

Josh replied, "Her dad's making sure she is."

"That's good. I've been thinking you look familiar, but can't think why."

"Me either. I'm a teacher, certainly not some personality."

"Maybe I'll figure it out before we get to KC," the man told him. "So, have you known your girlfriend a long time?"

Josh answered with, "Not really, we just sort of clicked at our first meeting," smiling as he remembered that day at the Pearsons'.

"That happens sometimes. Where'd you meet, with you being in Nebraska and her in Kansas?"

"You ever hear of TrailWays?" Josh asked.

"That's it! That's where I remember you from. Don't you do something for them in the summer?"

"Yeah, Pony Express Rider, for one."

"My family has been on treks a couple of times in the past," the man said. "And the Friday Nights. Don't they open up this weekend?"

"Yeah, I'm not sure yet whether I'll work any this year."

"Maybe I'll see you if you do."

~

Jerilyn wondered why the invitation from her dad, and why didn't she ask. Whatever the reason, it would present a good respite, since she told herself she still wasn't visiting him enough—especially since she might be moving hundreds of miles away. Then she crossed her fingers. *Hopefully moving.* Classes were over—both her teaching and her college class, though there would be meetings at school on Tuesday for teachers.

It was still a few weeks before her trip to Nebraska. She was grateful there had been more communication between her and Josh the last week or so, relieving a lot of the anxiety she felt. It would be so good when they could discuss plans face to face. Though she was still unsure what they might be, or when things might happen, hopefully leading to marriage. She had been afraid to even think about a permanent resolution.

When she reached her dad's house, Jerilyn noted that in addition to her brothers' cars, there was another one in the driveway. She was always glad to see Jack and Jon, but couldn't help wondering who the other vehicle belonged to—maybe Linda or Jayden?

~

Josh was nervously waiting. When he met Jerilyn's brothers, he noted they seemed to have something in mind they wanted to say to him. But Jeff noticed it also, and thought he probably knew what they were planning. He admonished them and asked how they would feel if Linda's or Jayden's relatives confronted them in the same way. They had only planned it as a teasing gesture, but realized their dad was right.

Instead, they told Josh they knew their sister was very much in love with him and they would be glad to have him in their family.

So it was a subdued atmosphere when Jerilyn entered the room.

"Hi, Jerilyn, remember me?"

Was it real, or were her thoughts so much on him, she only imagined he was there in front of her?

"Josh?" She didn't want to ask, she only wanted to feel his arms around her. They moved toward each other and were soon embracing, then hungrily kissing.

Jerilyn looked around the room at all the males, still holding onto Josh's hand. "I love this surprise, but how did it happen?"

Her dad did most of the telling—how Josh got in touch with him, then how it progressed from there. "I told him he could stay here with all of us guys, but I'm pretty sure he wants to stay with you."

"I do have that extra room, and if he's with me, we won't keep you all awake with our catching up."

Jon said, "And your kisses."

She looked at him, then Jack, and asked, "How old are you two anyway? Sometimes you act like a couple of kids."

"We are younger than you," from Jon.

Jack added, "And we did want to ask his intentions, but Dad stopped us."

At that, Josh laughed, "So that's what all that was about when I first arrived?"

"Yeah, and it's why we're in uniform. We wanted to appear more authoritative."

They were interrupted by Jeff, who told them, "If it's okay with you, we're going to order Chinese; any favorites?"

They told him no, whatever he ordered would be fine. Jon and Jack changed to civilian clothes before leaving to pick up the food.

"Like we said, the uniforms were to impress Josh. We don't go on duty 'til later."

"For whatever reason, I applaud you both on your choice of careers," Josh told them. "We certainly need more good people to follow your example. Though, unfortunately, the role of all first responders is becoming more dangerous than ever. I'm sure your dad and sister are proud of you."

As the brothers went out the door, Josh turned his attention to Jerilyn, gathering her close. They both needed another hug, and a kiss. Then they moved into the kitchen, taking seats and talking over each other, trying to catch up. Both were at the end of the school year and compared what the last days brought. She mentioned some of the things she learned in the class she took and told him the expectations for special ed teachers weren't that different.

She asked about the class she knew he planned to begin in a few days, and was surprised when Josh told her he had decided after all not to proceed with it at this time. He would tell her why later.

~

When they were eating, Jeff asked Josh, "Tell me a little about yourself, if you don't mind."

"Well, I think you know I'm a teacher, but have been helping out at TrailWays in the summers."

"I'd like to know more about that. I know some from what Jerilyn has shared. How long have you been involved?"

Jerilyn was interested in his answer too, since she had never asked.

"Mark Thomas and I went to high school together—he was a grade ahead of me, but we still were fairly good friends. When his folks 'retired' from ranching and started up Trail-Ways, he and I and his brother Matt helped on some of the trail rides. They weren't quite as complex as they are now.

"Then when they added the Pony Express I was ready, though there are still situations when I help with the treks."

"What about family?" Jeff asked.

"Dad was a rancher; his name was Andrew. He died several years ago, and we still miss him. Mom was a bank teller. Her name's Martha, but everyone knows her as Mat-tie. My only sibling is my sister Nancy, who's a bit younger than me. She's a Physical Therapist in Scottsbluff. So far, not married, not even sure there's ever been anyone serious in her life."

Turning to the boys, he said, "I heard one of you brothers is dating Austen's sister?"

Jon told him, "Yeah, me. Hasn't been long, but she's pretty special to me."

"How about you, Jack?"

"Just recently met a friend of Jerilyn's. I like her." At a look from his sister, he added, "a lot."

Jon chimed in, "Before he met her, he pretty much played the field."

Jack told him, "You're one to talk."

"Okay, you're right."

During their exchange of words, Jerilyn and her dad glanced at each other and shook their heads—typical dinner table conversation.

Glancing from Jeff to Jerilyn, Josh said, "I know Jeff retired as a Police Lieutenant, and know what you siblings do; what about your mother?"

"She worked for many years in the advertising department of the newspaper, doing everything from secretarial work to composing ads."

Jeff added, "She was working there when we got married. She took some time off and was able to be a stay-at-home mom 'til the kids were older. Then she went back to work at the same job for a few more years."

~

Beginning the weekend at Jeff's provided a good time for the Tates and Josh to become better acquainted and to learn more about their separate lives.

Jerilyn told him as they were leaving, "Thanks, Dad, for doing this."

"Well, you know, I thought it would be a good thing for all of us."

Josh came to where they were standing and said, "Yes, it has been."

Josh and Jerilyn left at the same time as her brothers, who had changed back into their uniforms. He followed behind as she drove to her house. When they got there, he carried his things to the room that would be his for a couple of days. As they walked through the house, they were both remembering when she stayed with him for Mark and Austen's wedding. In many ways, it felt like a lifetime ago.

She showed him through the rest of the house, then told him, "I was thinking we could take that tour of the city we talked about when you were here before. But it's been a long day for you and you're probably tired."

"Well, I'm not that old. But I would like to just relax and talk about us. Maybe we can do the tour tomorrow."

"Okay. Want to go to church with me in the morning? We would need to leave here at eight thirty."

He took a seat on the couch and said, "Sure, now come and sit with me. I need a hug and more kisses."

What began as that, a quick hug and a kiss, changed with their hunger for each other. He relaxed onto the couch, lying with her on top of him, wrapped as closely together as they could get. He began to turn over, his leg caught between hers. Her arms went around his shoulders and she began to pull him toward her, wanting to feel his lips on hers, when he stopped, sat upright, and pulled her to sit beside him, continuing to hold her.

"Sorry, didn't mean for that to happen. Maybe we should go sit at the table?"

She was surprised at her disappointment; she hadn't wanted him to stop—whatever it was going to be. She felt bereft, missing his touch.

When they were settled, he said, "There's something I need to tell you anyway."

Twelve

"Both my sister and Mark told me that I needed to tell you about something that happened about four years ago that I had actually forgotten about," Josh told her.

"Sherise Tracy blew into Plattsford with her family. One night they came to Friday Night Feed, and for some reason, she latched onto me. I learned later that Mark was the first to garner her attention, but it took little time for her to realize that was useless. It was immediately after his wife left, and you've heard how he was for years, certainly not open to another woman's attention.

"Sherise was what Kate called simpering. She would grab my arm and pull herself close to me with false smiles and compliments, acting helpless in certain situations, like a damsel in distress. And I was fooled. No female had ever acted like that around me and I didn't recognize the deceit in her actions. In my mind, she seemed to crave my attention and was with me as much as possible. It was summer, so there was plenty of time to spend with her.

"She told me she loved me, though there was no truth in it, and I was sure I was in love with her. I was planning to ask her to marry me, even looked at rings at a jewelry store in

Scottsbluff, then decided it would be better to choose them together.

"Nancy, Mark, and the Pearsons all knew what I was feeling; there may have been others; only my mother didn't know about her. When they talk about it, they call her my 'almost fiancée.'

"They all tried to warn me, telling me she was all show and no substance, but I thought they just didn't know her. Then suddenly, a couple of days before I planned to propose, the family was gone. None of us ever heard of, or from, the family again, so not sure about their history. It took me a while to realize how lucky I was, but I guess the experience did affect me; just not quite the same as Mark, but close.

"Then you came along," he finished.

She sat quietly as he related the story, but wanting to have her close to him, he pulled her out of her chair onto his lap.

"You haven't said anything. Has there been a similar experience for you?"

"What do you mean? Have I led anyone on?" she asked.

"No, has anyone treated you like that?"

Hesitating very briefly, she finally told him, "I've hardly had a boyfriend, let alone a relationship that might even appear to be serious."

Saying that, Jerilyn felt the need to release herself from his arms and took a seat away from him.

A memory did come to her mind. When she was in college, there was a boy in one of her classes. She was a junior, he a senior; there was a special, wonderful feeling of joyous exhilaration and even expectation when she was with him.

Maybe an early love, but nothing was ever said about a future together.

Then he graduated and went home, way back east. She never heard from him again. For years, some small thing would remind her of him and how desolate and forlorn she felt after he was no longer there.

She never shared any of that with her family. And now she wondered if that may have been the reason there was never a serious boyfriend. Had she closed up her heart?

Josh was surprised at her statement. "I can't believe that. Has every man been blind, or what?"

"I was a tomboy, and maybe my hair scared them; you know the color is an anomaly. A lot of guys don't like red hair."

"I think you're wrong. I bet there were plenty who worshipped you from afar."

"Yeah, more likely tolerated me like someone's pesky sister."

"Your beauty and confidence probably intimidated them. I love your beautiful auburn hair that frames your beautiful face. I want to wrap it around my hands and pull you closer for a kiss."

With that, he rose, then pulled her from her chair into his arms. "And I'm glad there's been no one else, so you can be mine."

"Well, you know, back in the day they would have called me an old maid schoolteacher. But though there hasn't been anyone I've had any particular interest in—whether or not anyone was interested in me—I have dreamed of being married and having a family, wondering what 'he' would look like, how we would meet, where we would live."

"I hope I fit into those dreams."

Josh wanted to assure her of her worth, of his love for her. A love that would be everlasting. How lucky that it was he who met her at TrailWays.

They returned to the living room and the couch. "Because I want you close," he said.

"I have to be honest," Jerilyn told him. "It would never have occurred to me that I would meet a man from Nebraska. Who goes to Nebraska?" she asked with a grin.

"Nor I a woman from Kansas. Who goes to Kansas?"

"Yet here we are."

"Okay, I'm changing the subject," Jerilyn said. "What happened to your plans for a class this summer?"

"I had a talk with Mark." At her questioning look, he continued. "He pointed out how much time it would take, that even when you come to visit, I would be away. The most important thing is you. And I can always do it later. It was his idea that I make the trip this weekend."

"Well, bless Mark," she said.

"And Austen. She told him he needed to talk to me. And so he did, and so I'm here."

"What shall we do with all this time?"

"Maybe it's a good chance to learn more about each other, and how we came to be who we are?"

"Okay, you go first. You told us that your dad was a rancher. So how did you come to be a teacher instead?"

"I loved living on the ranch, and didn't even mind the hard work, but my mom and dad struggled to keep everything together. And overhearing them discussing finances made me start to ponder something else. My mom was earning a little. I think without that we would have lost it. There were a couple of teachers I admired who influenced me. They assisted me in getting scholarships and even some jobs to help me afford college.

"I know Dad was disappointed I wasn't going to stay in ranching—his father was the one who bought the land and started the legacy. But he also understood. Then he learned he had cancer. He died my second year at the university. My brilliant sister received so much in scholarships they almost covered the entire cost of earning her bachelor's and completing her physical therapy training.

"I'm sorry to say, I wasn't thinking about how much my mom's life changed. And probably I still haven't. Need to correct that when I get home. She was a ranch kid too but has taken to town life okay. Dad had a little insurance, and sale of the ranch made it possible for her to quit her job."

"You do know that our lives have been almost completely opposite?" Jerilyn asked. "I've always lived in town, never been on a horse, except that time when you took me back to TrailWays' headquarters."

"But you are a teacher too."

"Yes, there's that."

"I've been doing most of the talking," Josh said. "And I guess I do know quite a bit about you from your dad and brothers and Austen. Anything else you want to tell me?"

Grinning, she said, "No, you can just learn as we go along."

~

It had been a full day, and by the time Josh finished recounting his life and experiences it was early evening. They ordered pizza for supper, thinking of the Thomas family, especially David, who seemed to always be ready for one more bite.

After the meal, they settled into a soft, warm atmosphere, content with sitting together, holding hands, sharing more about their childhoods. Mentioning her brothers, she told him, "Although I'm older, from a young age they paired up to 'protect me' from everything, including any boys who might show an interest. Maybe that's the reason I never had a serious relationship."

"I may have done the same thing with Nancy," Josh said. "I am older, and remember my folks always instructing me to 'take care of her.' I hope that didn't happen, but she's still single too. I think you two will like each other. I haven't kept in touch with her as much as I should, though she's only as far away as Scottsbluff."

Jerilyn didn't want to break the spell by mentioning bedtime, especially since she was beginning to feel a bit awkward. She didn't remember feeling that way at his home when she was there for Austen's wedding. How did they handle that evening?

She stood up anyway, telling him, "I don't know what time you got up this morning, but I'm beginning to wilt, and I didn't even have to catch a plane. Now, much as I'd like to stay up, it's my bedtime."

She began straightening up the room and turning off the lights.

Josh admitted, "Yeah, I'm a bit wilted too. It was an early beginning for me, so I'll take myself off to bed. Not sure I'll sleep; will be thinking about you in the same house with me. But I definitely need a good-night kiss. Then I'll walk you to your door."

"It should be the other way around, since you're my guest."

"That would be okay too. Maybe you'll decide to tuck me in?"

Just the thought caused a sensation in her stomach and an increased heartbeat. "That's probably not a good idea. I might not want to leave."

Why did she say that out loud? Their eyes caught; it was as if he were thinking the same thing.

"I'll let you off this time, but I still want a kiss."

She didn't need any more urging, letting him draw her into his arms, simply hugging for a while. "It's been such a good day. I love being here with you."

Then came the kiss they both wanted. They were standing in front of the door to the room he was using, and he whispered against her lips, "I love you so much."

Then he quickly opened the door and went in, closing it quietly behind him.

It had been quite an eventful day which began with his unexpected appearance, so she wondered if there would be any rest for her. Despite her concern, tired as she was, she was asleep after only a few minutes. She remembered later there were vague dreams, but no details came to mind.

~

Jerilyn hadn't thought about breakfast until Sunday morning. For herself, that usually meant coffee and toast made from her favorite sunflower-seed bread. A pot of coffee was started, and she was checking the cabinets for any other possibilities when Josh walked in. His jeans were on, but not fastened, and he was pulling on a shirt.

His bare chest drew her eyes; and at the same time she was checking him out, he was filling his eyes with her: hair still tousled, no makeup and sweats, each wanting to wrap their arms around the other.

"Do you usually sleep in sweats, or is it just for me?"

"Don't you think they're sexy?" she asked.

Moving toward her, his shirt on but not yet buttoned, he told her, "Yes, anything you wear is sexy," and succumbed to the impulse to gather her close for a good-morning kiss.

She first ran her hands over his unshaved face, then her arms went around him, touching his bare skin, as the kiss deepened.

His mouth not really leaving hers, he said, "You're beautiful in the morning."

After a few minutes Jerilyn pulled away from him and said, "We've got to end this if we're going to church. I was checking to see if I have anything for breakfast."

"What do you usually have?"

"Toast and coffee."

"Then that's okay for me too."

There were a few awkward moments as they got ready for church. Neither was accustomed to having another person around, let alone one of the opposite sex, as they showered and dressed. Usually there was no need to be concerned about being covered up.

~

They looked each other up and down as they came out of their rooms. Jerilyn told him, "Be prepared for a lot of second glances when we get there. Dad and my brothers are the only ones besides me who know you're here."

"I think I can handle it."

Just as she expected, there was quite a stir as they walked in, especially among her group of friends.

Maggie was the first to see them, and brought her husband with her to say hello to Josh.

"Hi, I'm Maggie; don't know whether you remember me? When I was in Nebraska with Jerilyn, you only had eyes for her."

"Yes, I do—barely," he told her with a grin.

"This is my husband, Terry. Our kids are already in their class."

While the two men were shaking hands, others of her group gathered around them, including Jayden.

Some asked Jerilyn why she hadn't told them he would be there.

"Since I didn't know he was coming, I couldn't very well tell you. He did get in touch with my dad so he would be sure I would be home," glancing at Jayden, who nodded her head.

When they questioned her, Jayden told them Jack had let her know. "I probably knew before Jerilyn did."

Josh was still standing beside her and finally said, "Are you going to introduce me to your friends?"

"Of course, sorry. This is Jayden, Jack's girlfriend. You know Maggie—and meet Merritt and Lainie."

He shook hands with each one, then took Jerilyn's hand as she finished.

"You've probably guessed this is Josh."

"We've heard a lot about you. How long are you going to be here?"

"Just until tomorrow. School again on Tuesday."

Jeff and Jack entered the church and acknowledged the group; Jon was still on his forty-eight-hour shift. Jack took Jayden's hand as they left to find a seat and the others scattered to their usual places.

Jerilyn, Josh, and her dad selected seats together. During the opening praise service, Josh joined in, making her wonder if he might be a regular part of the TrailWays' band, reminding her there was still a lot she didn't know about him.

It was different having him beside her. He had reached his arm around her, resting it on the back of the pew, then shifted and took her hand, holding it through most of the service.

Thirteen

As they were leaving church, Jerilyn asked, "Dad, want to come for coffee? Not sure about lunch yet."

He received a text from Josh before they left for church and thought her invitation would work into whatever was on Josh's mind, so said, "Sure." She didn't notice the silent communication between the two men, with Josh nodding "yes."

She started a fresh pot of coffee as soon as she and Josh got to her house and brought out some cookies. Josh hugged and kissed her, then told her he needed some time with her dad.

She gave a questioning look to both of them, wondering what about, having no idea he was sweetly following an old tradition. But she said, "Okay," and left the room.

"Jeff, maybe you can guess why I requested this meeting? I believe you know I love your daughter very much; so much I can hardly contain it, and I'm sure she feels the same. I've been so thankful we got back together after the emptiness of the past fall and winter. She and I haven't specifically talked about marriage, but our eventual life together has been hinted at in many ways.

"Right now, I don't know where our future will be—Nebraska or here. I haven't asked her yet, but I'm asking you for her hand in marriage, and for your blessing."

They were sitting at the table, somehow the most natural and comfortable spot for their conversation. When Josh finished his request, Jeff reached for his hand. As he shook it, he said, "Thank you for this. It means a lot. I've heard enough from Jerilyn to know she loves you too. And I've seen you, and been around you enough, that I believe I can make a good judgment. I'm happy to give my consent and pray for the best for you as you both make plans for your future together. I will be honored to be your father-in-law."

~

After their conversation, Josh went looking for Jerilyn. He found her leafing through a family scrapbook. He took it from her, hoping to see images of her when she was a little girl. It was open to a picture of her family.

"This must be your mother. She's beautiful, just like you. And how cute you were."

His finger traced around the face of the girl in the picture, wondering what a child of his and Jerilyn's might look like.

"Yes, she was beautiful; we all still miss her. So, did you men get everything taken care of?" she asked as they returned to the kitchen.

Both nodded, then poured second cups of coffee, asking her to join them.

"Are you going to tell me, or is it a secret?" Jerilyn asked.

"When the time is right."

Whatever that means, she thought.

There was some discussion about the church service and all the people Josh had met. "I enjoyed it all, and you have some great friends."

"Yes, I do."

Then she told him, "Since I wasn't expecting company, I really don't have anything to make much of a meal—lunch or supper. I usually just grab something from the freezer or open a can of soup."

"There must be some favorite place to eat out?"

"Sure, Cinzetti's; it's an Italian buffet."

"Why don't we go there then—say mid-afternoon, and that could take care of both meals. Maybe Jeff can join us."

"No, thanks. I like the place too, but I think you two need to enjoy your time together."

He left shortly afterward, leaving them alone to contemplate how to spend the rest of the day.

For a while, they just looked at each other, then moved into a kiss, with Josh saying, "I'm so glad Mark convinced me I should make this trip. It's going to be hard leaving you tomorrow. Wish you could just come with me."

"Me too." Then, "This is nice, but we can't do this all day."

"Why not?"

"I've promised a tour of the city a couple of times and it hasn't happened yet. Maybe we can do that?"

"Actually, sounds kind of boring to me. Is there a certain spot that you like to visit?"

"There is the Arboretum. I don't get to go there often, and it being a holiday weekend, may be busy."

"Let's go there anyway. I'll let you drive, so you won't have to give me directions."

"Okay. I'll change to jeans."

~

As they drove toward Metcalf, Jerilyn told him, "It's about fifteen miles to the Gardens; and it's been in existence less than thirty years, so it's almost new when you compare it to others around the country. It was a favorite of my mother. As I told you, I don't get to go as often as I would like, but once I'm there, it's hard to leave, it's so restful. Maybe that should remind me I don't relax enough?"

"Don't think I've ever visited an Arboretum or Botanical Garden, so it will be a new experience for me," Josh replied.

~

They wandered through the gardens, following the trails and nature walks, noting the life-size statues in the Sculpture Garden, but mostly just enjoying the ambience and environment of the place. Josh agreed with her that it provided a most tranquil experience.

There were several areas, including waterfalls among the trees, some flowering, and others with emerging new leaves. The water was tumbling over large boulders, with others around as sort of barriers, arranged in such a natural way that the falls could have always been there.

He noted a bench near one of them and said, "Let's sit here. Sure is a nice day, perfect for a visit. But you need more than an hour or two to see everything."

"Yes, some spots deserve at least an hour of their own."

After they were settled, resting for a while, Josh moved to his knee in front of her, then took her hand.

"Jerilyn Tate, I think I've loved you since I first saw you, then asked you to ride behind me on that horse. I could hardly bear those months when not only were we not together, we weren't communicating. It's still hard to be apart, but I hope that won't be much longer."

Tears were streaming down her face.

"Will you marry me, so we can be together for always?"

"Yes, yes, yes, Josh Wilson. I love you too."

He sat back on the bench with her, holding her in a loving hug, then initiating one of his kisses she seemed to be always craving. People walking by had seen the proposal, some even waiting to learn the answer. They believed someone even took a picture.

"By the way, that coffee session with your dad was to ask his permission."

"Oh, who would have thought you would be so thoughtful?" she asked.

Which brought Josh to ask, "You don't believe I can be thoughtful?"

"That's not what I meant, but you have to remember, we're still learning about each other. How many days has it been that we've actually been together? Probably not even a week."

Saying that, they briefly pulled apart, looking into each other's eyes, then, arms around each other again, decided that was long enough.

They took notice of this particular spot, knowing that from then on it would be a special place for them, then returned to the trail headed toward the parking lot.

Josh told her, "I don't have a ring yet. Maybe we can pick one out when you come to visit me. And I realize there's lots to think about, planning a wedding, even where we're going to live. But I hope it won't be long."

The first thing both did after entering Jerilyn's home was to start texting Mark and Austen Thomas, even before contacting their families.

From Jerilyn: "Thank you so much for your part in Josh's trip. He proposed, I said yes. Many plans ahead of us."

And from Josh: "Did I thank you for prodding me to visit Jerilyn? If not, I'm sorry. It's been a great visit. I proposed, she said yes."

Mark and Austen received the texts at the same time and turned to each other, saying, "Guess what?"

The couple put their phones down and wrapped their arms around each other.

Austen told him, "I hope they will be as happy as we are. I'm so in love with you, it hurts sometimes."

"I hope the same," Mark said. "I still ask myself why it took so long for me to admit I loved you and wanted to be with you for always."

Then came the kiss that never failed to fill her with warmth throughout her whole being. And as they continued to hold each other, they both felt the baby kick, bringing smiles.

"Seems like 'baby' is reminding us it's TrailWays' season and we still have things to do before tomorrow." Then Mark gave her another sweet kiss, put his hat on, and started out the door.

Turning back, he said, "Just think, it was a year ago that we had our first training session. Any regrets?"

"You know there aren't," Austen told him. "Anything you need help with?"

"Not today; we'll see about tomorrow when tomorrow comes."

They eventually texted back to Jerilyn and Josh with congratulations.

~

Instead of texting, Jerilyn called her dad. "I know this is no surprise to you, but Josh proposed. Of course, I said yes."

"Congratulations. So, any wedding plans?"

"No. I'm sure you know there's a lot to think about," she said. "We'll probably talk more when I'm there in a couple of weeks."

"That makes sense."

"Thanks for being such a great dad. Don't know whether I've ever said that before. I love you, Dad."

"Love you too."

"I'll talk to you later. Have a few more people I want to contact. Bye."

"Bye."

~

While she was talking to her dad, Josh called his mother.

"Hi, Mom. Wanted to let you know I proposed to Jerilyn and she accepted."

When she didn't answer, he asked, "Are you okay?"

"Yes, I guess I'm just a bit surprised," his mother told him. "Even though you told me how important she is to you, think I was expecting it would be a while before considering a marriage. Even if you are getting older." He could tell she was smiling.

"I know you and Dad dated for a long time. But you got to see each other nearly every day. I want Jerilyn where I can see her—every day. And it's going to be in the same house, wherever that happens to be."

"Is she still going to be here in a few weeks?"

"Yes, and obviously there's still lots to plan. I'll be home tomorrow, so will call and we can talk more. Love you."

"Love you too, Son."

After talking to their parents, they really didn't want to contact anyone else yet. Instead, they moved to the couch, wanting to be close. They didn't mention it, but both were already dreading the coming day when Josh would be leaving.

Then Jerilyn said, "You know we still haven't had lunch. What time is it anyway?"

"Not sure I'm even hungry for food. Maybe we can just fill up on love."

"Sounds good, but not sure that would hold you, or me, 'til breakfast. But instead of our original plan, how about someplace else? Do you like Mexican?"

"Have to say I'm not sure. But I'm willing to try it."

"There's a restaurant not too far from here. And maybe it will provide a more intimate atmosphere."

~

When they were home after their meal, a short time was spent discussing her upcoming trip to Nebraska. But as they were sitting together on her couch, that soon changed. Josh's arms went around her, pulling her as close as possible.

"Jerilyn; do you have any idea how I love that name?" Then against her lips, "How I love saying that name. I'm so glad I made this trip. I already knew I loved you, but being able to hold you and kiss you—" at this, he stopped talking to give her one of those kisses that reached deep, and filled her with longing for more.

He pulled her on top of him, and she moved, trying to get closer. Pulling her lips from his, she began kissing his face, then moved down to his neck, then with a realization of her actions, sat up.

"Not sure this is such a good idea. Maybe I should stay with your mother when I'm there."

"I do want you to stay in my arms forever, but I promise I'll be good if you stay with me. Maybe."

Fourteen

When morning came, Jerilyn reminded both of them there still was nothing more for breakfast than coffee and toast.

"I know I haven't planned and prepared a meal for you since you've been here. Unless you count toast and coffee. You'll think I don't know how to. And I must admit, I don't very often, since there's just me."

"Doesn't matter whether you can or not. I love you anyway," Josh told her. "And I didn't give you advance notice. So, it's probably just as much my fault."

Jerilyn said, "First Watch is a good place for breakfast, and their menu offers many wonderful dishes. Besides that, it's close."

"Okay, let's go."

~

While they were enjoying their breakfast, several of Jerilyn's friends came in. Even though she planned to, she still had not contacted them about her engagement. But Jayden knew, and the news quickly passed from one to the other. They were disappointed she had no ring to show them. Some admitted they would probably want 'their guy' to have picked one out himself, even if it needed to be adjusted later. She made note that Jayden was included in the group who felt that way.

Seeing the distressed look on Josh's face, they told him, "But it's probably more practical to pick it out together. At least we'd be sure to get something we liked."

Josh told them, "Well, in my defense, I planned this trip at the last minute, was thinking mostly about just seeing Jerilyn."

~

The time for Josh to leave came too soon for them both. There still had been no actual discussion about a wedding, and when they could be together permanently. She was expecting that would occur when she was visiting him. Especially since they were going to shop for rings while she was there.

Partings were becoming more difficult, and she wasn't sure she could bear another one, let alone knowing there would be more than one. Maybe while she was in Nebraska, she would suggest an elopement? But that might require going someplace else. Could a couple get married immediately any place except Las Vegas?

She clung to him before he got into the car to drive away. "I'm so glad you came, but it hasn't been long enough."

"It's going to be hard waiting for you to come to me."

With one last kiss, he closed his door and started the drive toward the airport. She waved until the car turned at the corner and was soon out of sight.

Then not wanting to be by herself, she called her dad to find out if she could stop by to see him.

"I'm always glad to have you visit. Come on over."

He sensed she was despondent about Josh's departure, and was waiting at the door when she arrived, taking her into his arms for support.

"Oh, Dad. It's getting harder being apart from him; and I can't see that changing soon, even though I'll be there in a few weeks. And some of the things we'll have to decide will mean separation from family for one of us."

"You'll be a new family, and that needs to come first," her dad told her. "But you're right, you two will have to make that decision; no one else should be involved. I love you very much, and if you end up in Nebraska, I'll miss you. But we can keep in touch, and it will be a new place for me to visit."

"You're so wise."

"Don't they say, older and wiser? If not, they should. Would be terrible if knowledge didn't increase with age and experience. Now how about some lunch?" he asked.

"Okay, then I really need to go to the grocery store. There's hardly anything in my refrigerator."

She was glad neither of her brothers was there, though she always enjoyed visiting with them and hearing their news. And she wanted to ask if one of them would stay at her house during her trip to Nebraska. Maybe one would even want to buy it if she ended up moving, especially if they might be thinking of marriage too, though she had lived there alone for the past few years. It was probably time for them to be on their own, but what would that mean for her father? She hadn't thought about it before, but they might have chosen to stay with him on purpose to allay his loneliness.

~

Josh was already seated when the same guy he met on the way to KC came down the plane's aisle and took the seat next to him.

"Hey, it's you again. How was your visit with your girlfriend?"

"I proposed, she accepted."

"That's good. So, when's the wedding, and where?"

"No date yet, lots to think about. One of us will have to move. She'll be visiting me in a few weeks; probably be more definite plans after that."

"I can see there will be lots of planning. Congratulations, anyway."

"Don't think we exchanged names on the last flight. I'm Josh Wilson."

"Mitchell Robbins. Wilson—I've been going to physical therapy lately for my shoulder. One of the therapists is Nancy Wilson. I don't suppose she's any relation?"

"My sister."

"Wow, guess it is a small world. Is she married, engaged—serious boyfriend?"

"Not married, never been married. As far as I know, no one special in her life right now."

It was apparent to Josh the man held more interest in his sister than just as a therapist.

"You've probably guessed she's caught my attention," Mitchell said. "I've flirted, sort of my nature, but no more than that. And of course, she knows my name. After all, I am a patient."

"I was one of those flirts too," Josh told him. "So, what's your story? How come you need PT?"

"Injured my shoulder, roping."

"So, you a cowboy?" Josh asked.

"Guess you could say that. Actually, have a ranch with my folks where we raise calves for the rodeo. And I compete too. Beginning to think I'm getting too old for it, but it's always been part of my life. Any idea what your sister might think of that?"

"Can't say I do. Our family were ranchers too. I remember going to rodeos a couple of times when we were kids."

"Does your family still own a ranch?"

"No. My dad died. Neither Nancy nor I were interested in maintaining that lifestyle, though it was great growing up there. Anyway, Mom sold the ranch. She lives in Plattsford now, not far from me."

"Does that mean you don't think she would want to live on a ranch again? That sounds preemptive. Sorry."

"It's okay, think I understand. And I don't know how she might feel about returning to that life."

After those words, Mitchell seemed to withdraw into himself, perhaps pondering the possibility of getting to know Nancy better.

~

When he was seated in his pickup at the airport, Josh sent a text to Jerilyn before starting home.

"Did I mention the guy I met on the plane on way to KC? He was on the return trip too and we sat together again. Lots to tell you, too much for a text; will call tonight. I want to hear your voice anyway. Love you."

He then called his mother.

"Hi, Mom. Back in Scottsbluff, thought maybe I'd stop by to see you before going on home."

"Anita is here."

"Why?"

"I told her you'd probably be stopping by. She wants to see you."

"She's not going to see me, Mom, nor you either today, I guess. I'll call you when I get home." Then he hung up before she could say more.

Starting the pickup and heading toward home, Josh was thinking his mother must not have grasped how important Jerilyn was to him, though he had told her he proposed. What was it going to take to convince her of that? Why was she still influenced by Anita? From what he could tell, Anita didn't really like his mother and only continued to polish the friendship because of her unfound hopes of a relationship with him.

He was really bothered by the situation. Jerilyn was going to be Mattie's daughter-in-law and it was important to him that they have a good relationship. He hoped his mother would realize that and prepare herself for welcoming Jerilyn when she came. And to be honest, he hoped by then Anita would have smartened up and even left the area. Should he ask Austen for help?

~

"Hello, I'm home."

"I miss you already."

"Yeah, me too."

He told her about Mitchell Robbins and how he seemed to have a crush on his sister. "I'll probably not mention it to her, but I have a feeling I'm going to hear more about this man. What did you do this afternoon?"

"Went to see my dad, then to the grocery store. Don't you think it was about time?" she asked with a smile in her voice.

"Well, maybe. Really, I had enough to eat. Your kisses filled me up."

"That couldn't last forever."

"Maybe not, but I'm willing to try. Guess I should call my mother. Wish you were with me."

"Me too. Love you."

"Love you."

~

Bracing himself, Josh called his mother. If Anita were still there, he wouldn't talk to her.

"Hello."

"Is Anita still there?"

"No."

"Did you invite her, or did she just show up on her own?"

"I saw her at church yesterday. When she asked about you, I told her you were gone for the weekend."

"Did you tell her why?"

"No."

"Why not? Don't you remember what I told you about her? I don't like her; I have never liked her, not even as a friend. Just tried to be nice because I felt sorry for her. There was only one reason I was gone—Jerilyn. Wish I had just stayed there, except I do have to finish school. I love her so much it hurts. And I feel lost every day without her. You need to accept she is going to be your daughter-in-law. I'm sorry I didn't get to come by to see you. Maybe at the end of the day tomorrow. I do love you, Mom. And I want you and Jerilyn to love each other. So, please open your heart for her. She'll be here for a visit, and I hope Anita will be nowhere around."

"Love you too, son. Guess I need to be a little more assertive where Anita's concerned. I do remember what you told me, and I'm anxious to meet Jerilyn. I can tell how much you love her just by the way you say her name."

He hadn't told Nancy that Jerilyn accepted his proposal, and as he started a text to her, he recalled his visit with Mitchell Robbins on the plane.

"You probably heard that I'm engaged. Need to plan a visit with you when she's here. How about you—anyone special?"

He debated when, if ever, he would mention Mitchell.

He received a return text from her as he was organizing what he would need for the last day of school.

"Congratulations. I'm looking forward to meeting my 'almost' sister-in-law. No one special. Love you."

~

The weeks before Jerilyn's trip to Nebraska passed slowly for them. There was little to occupy her time, but much on her mind. She wouldn't know for a while whether she would be staying in Kansas or moving, so thought it would be good to consider what to do with many of the things she had accumulated in the last few years. Some needed to be discarded or donated, whatever the decision was. It was a good time for "cleaning out."

While she was standing amid the items, her brother Jack knocked, then came on in. "Hey, Sis, looks like you're planning to move."

"Don't know yet. Hopefully, I will know by the time I return from Nebraska. Just going through things I don't use, or wear, or need anymore. They need to be purged either way. I'm glad you stopped by. How are things going with you now that you're officially a police officer?"

"Mostly routine stuff. You may not know that a lot of an officer's life is boredom. Nothing exciting yet, but guess I better not complain; I'm sure there will be plenty of that."

"I wanted to ask you boys if one of you would be able to stay here while I'm gone. Kind of hate to leave the house empty for that long."

"I should be able to. Besides, if you end up moving to Nebraska, you'll probably want to sell, and maybe I would be interested in buying. Could bring Jayden by to get her thoughts."

"Are you that serious?"

"I'm feeling pretty serious; sorry to say, I don't know about her. You know, she's kind of quiet. But she seems to like me a lot." The last said with a smile.

"Are you going to ask Jon, or should I talk to him?"

"I'll mention it, then maybe you two can figure it out and let me know?"

The same thought about going through things occurred to Josh, and Mark was surprised to see a pile of belongings in the living room when he stopped by one day.

"So, are you moving?"

"Don't know yet, but maybe. Even if I don't, I need to get rid of some of these things. How come people accumulate so much stuff? But I still don't know what to do with it."

"There is Community Services. They would even come pick it up."

"Sounds good. So, what are you doing here?"

"I know Jerilyn is going to be here, but not for several days. Just wondered if you'd be willing to help on some treks the end of the week?"

"Yeah. I need something physical to make the days pass more quickly."

Fifteen

"Hello, how are your days?" Jerilyn was glad to hear Josh's voice.

"Passing too slowly. Yours?"

"The same," Josh told her. "But Mark asked if I could help with some treks. I'll be doing one on Sunday afternoon, then an overnight one Monday. Figured it would be good to have some physical work."

"I understand that. Wish there were something besides housecleaning to get me through the days."

"I keep thinking about last summer and how Mark spent so much time avoiding or trying to avoid Austen. He was in love with her, even though he wouldn't admit it. Don't know how he got through the days without even kissing her. If that had been you and me, I would have wanted to get married immediately so I could spend all my time with you."

"So how are we going to get through the weeks when I am with you?" Jerilyn asked.

"May not be easy," he admitted. "It just convinces me we'll need to be ready to make some decisive plans for our wedding, and where we'll live, meaning, also, which of us will move. And I know that alone isn't going to be uncomplicated."

"You're right. But let's leave that until I'm there."

"Guess you've figured out I'm missing you so much," Josh told her. "And, since I'm going to be on those treks, you might not remember, if you ever knew, that we don't have our phones with us. If you need to get in touch with me, you can probably contact Austen."

Jerilyn admitted, "Oh. Just knowing I won't be able to reach you immediately will make it harder. I'm so glad you called; I've missed hearing your voice. So be careful on the treks, and don't flirt with anyone."

"I will, and I won't. Love you."

"Love you too. Bye."

"Bye."

~

Each day seemed to be longer than the one before for them both, convincing them even more that their wedding needed to be soon. It was getting harder to be apart. But there was much to consider.

Jack and Jon discussed which of them would stay at Jerilyn's while she was gone. Considering their work shifts, they concluded that Jack should do it since he was currently on the day shift. He came by with Jayden to get any instructions from his sister.

Jayden told her, "I've been here many times, but only in the living room, kitchen, and bathroom."

"Yes, we don't tend to do house tours when our group meets."

"Well, I'm her brother," Jack said, then turning to Jerilyn, "and I can't say I've been in your whole house either."

"Can't think of any reason why you would have needed to. Except, if you remember, you did help me move in."

"But the rooms were empty."

As they moved through the house, she kept an eye on them—Jack's arm around Jayden's shoulder, occasionally drawing her close for a kiss, then taking her hand. Watching them, she felt a prick of jealousy. They could take time for their love to grow.

Her relationship with Josh began with separation, making everything more intense when they were together. And as she thought about it, those times were still fewer than those Jack and Jayden were already enjoying.

In her eyes, it seemed Jack had matured in the past few weeks. He no longer seemed to be the teasing brother from spring break. She could never have imagined those two becoming a couple, but they appeared to be perfect for each other.

When they finished checking out all the rooms, Jerilyn asked if they had any questions.

Jack asked, "Is there anything off limits? Do I need to bring my own groceries? Do you expect me to clean?"

Jerilyn told him, "Regarding your last question, I don't expect you to clean, but I do expect you to keep things neat and if you make a mess, clean it up."

"Yeah, you're probably thinking back when I was just a kid. I'm a grown man now."

Maybe she was wrong after all about that teasing brother.

"Nothing is really off limits. If there's anything here you need, you're welcome to it. But don't leave the cabinets empty. And no wild parties."

Looking at Jayden and taking her hand, he told his sister, "If there were ever wild parties, they're definitely in the past; and I don't think the Chief would approve." Then continued, "I like your house, sis, the way you've furnished it makes it warm and welcoming. I might not want to leave when you get home."

~

Josh called her as soon as he finished the overnight trek.

"Hello."

"Hi, it's me."

"Yes. How were the treks?"

"Good. The one on Sunday afternoon was with a family, mom and dad and two boys. It was their first time, though they had heard a lot about TrailWays. They may plan a longer one later, and I believe they'll come for one of the Friday Night Feeds.

"The overnight trek was with people who have been coming every other year for quite some time. They remembered a lot, so didn't require a lot of instruction. Think they could almost be in charge of one themselves.

"What have you been doing?" he asked.

"My brothers decided Jack would stay here while I'm gone. He and Jayden came by for any instructions I might have for them, and to go through the house. And I've been going through my clothes, thinking about what I'll need for my visit with you. Mostly jeans?"

"Probably. And you know we do have stores here in case you need to get something else. Do you have boots?"

"No. Never thought I would need such a thing. Maybe I'll get a hat too?"

"Sounds good to me. Meantime, I'll be picturing you in western gear. Think you'll be pretty cute. And now, just thinking about that I want to reach out and touch you. I know it's only a few more days now, but seems so long since I was with you. And to think, there'll be another separation after that. Don't know how I'll be able to stand it."

"Yes, hard for me too."

"Don't want to say goodbye, but I really need a shower. Love you."

"Love you too."

~

Finally, it was the day for her to head for Nebraska. Thinking about how she might feel when she returned home—probably depressed and miserable—and not wanting to drive home alone, she asked her father if he could provide transportation to the airport and back. He didn't have to mull it over; he was always glad to spend time with her. And in the back of his mind was the thought that it was likely she would be moving to Nebraska before much more time elapsed.

On the way to the airport, he asked, "So have you two discussed when you'll be getting married, and where?"

"No. Everything is so complicated. Sometimes I would just like to elope, but I want you all with me. And there's also the question of where we'll live."

"You've got two weeks. I'm sure you'll have a better idea before that time is up. Have you considered the possibility of moving to Nebraska?"

"Actually, I have. And I need these coming days to learn more about what it's like. But to be honest, Dad, it's getting harder to be separated and I just want to be where he is. Is that being too idealistic?"

"I don't think so. That's the way your mom and I were."

"I miss her."

"Me too. Some days are still hard to get through," he said with sadness in his voice.

Before she got out of the car at the airport, her dad told her, "I think I've been around Josh enough to say he's probably feeling the same as you about wanting to be where you are. Hope you can get that worked out. Tell him 'hi' for me; have a great visit. I love you."

"Love you too, Dad."

~

When Josh and Jerilyn reached each other, it was almost as if it had been months since they were together instead of a few weeks—days, really. Others noticed as they gazed into each other's eyes and caressed the other's face as if getting reacquainted. Then at last wrapped their arms around each other for the kiss they craved. The longer they were apart, the hungrier they were for each other. How could they bear any more separations?

Their lips hardly apart, Josh told her, "I'm so glad you're here."

"So am I."

"I want you in my arms forever," he said, and pulled her closer, if that was possible.

Finally, he stepped back slightly and said, "Guess we need to move," as he realized they were in the way of other passengers.

He picked up her carry-on bag and took her hand as they moved toward the baggage carousel.

"How much luggage do you have?"

"Just one more bag," she told him.

"A bit different than when you came before. Will you be able to handle it?"

"Yes."

"Okay, I'll take this one and get the pickup and meet you out front."

~

Josh drove up just as Jerilyn came out. He noticed a young man who was looking admiringly at Jerilyn, then realized it was the man from the plane. As he stepped out of the pickup to help her, Mitchell also noticed him.

"Hey, it's you. Is this your girlfriend?"

"Yes. Jerilyn, meet Mitchell Robbins. So, are you flying to Kansas City again?"

"No, just came to see a friend off. He's going to a rodeo in Texas. It's good to see you again, and glad to meet you, Jerilyn."

Josh asked, "Are you still in therapy?"

"Yeah, otherwise it would be me on the plane." With a grin he added, "But I do still get to see your sister."

He turned to head to the parking area and told them, "Hope you have a great visit."

As he moved out of sight, Jerilyn asked, "So have you told Nancy about him?"

"No, not sure I will. What do you think?"

"I don't know your sister. He seems nice enough, but how can one know from such a brief meeting?"

"Our meeting was brief. But that moment I saw you at the Pearsons', I knew I wanted to know all about you. Actually, I wanted to take your hand and go someplace away from everyone else.

"That feeling scared me, how strongly I felt and all I could do was my usual flirting. Yeah, there was that almost fiancée I told you about, but I think that was just an ego thing—this girl chasing me. Looking back, it was like a grade-school crush which I never experienced."

"I bet there were girls who had a crush on you."

She thought back to that first time she saw Josh, and his being introduced as the Pony Express Rider. Her friend Maggie who made the trip to TrailWays with her asked later what she thought of him. Jerilyn had replied, "He's pretty cute, but think I need to be around him more to make any deeper comment."

"I never told you how glad I was to get that text from you after you left," Josh said.

"I was crying when I sent it, so was happy you texted back. And yet it was so long before our first kiss."

"Kind of hard to kiss when you're in different states."

"Yes," she agreed, but thinking how long it had been that way, and hoped after this trip, there would be a solution to that.

Sixteen

When they were on the highway headed to Plattsford, Josh asked, "Is it okay if we go by my mother's before going on to my place?"

"Does she know we might stop by?"

"Yes. I don't want to wait any longer for you two to meet; and when we get home, I want to stay."

"Okay, that sounds good." What else could she say? But she would have liked to have a bit more time to prepare. "You've never said much about your mother. Is there anything I should know?"

Why was she so concerned? It had always been easy for her to meet new people. There were new students with their parents every fall. But this was Josh's mother—quite a different circumstance. She had heard there were occasional times when a mother felt a special attachment to her son and might try to hinder any relationship he wanted to make permanent.

She was more than likely just borrowing trouble. *Happy thoughts, Jerilyn, happy thoughts.*

"She knows I love you."

At a look from her, he continued, "She's a sweet, friendly woman. Being a bank teller for several years, she's met nearly everyone in town. They like her too. It was hard for her when Dad died, and we sold the ranch. But she took to town life okay, maybe because she was already working at the bank.

"Frankly, to be honest, I need to tell you that I think she's jealous of all her friends who have grandchildren. She keeps reminding Nancy and me that we're getting older, probably a subtle or not so subtle hint that so is she."

Sensing her apprehension, Josh reached for her hand, hoping to allay any disquiet about the coming meeting with his mother. As they drove into the driveway at his mother's home, he looked over at Jerilyn and noted there was still concern in her eyes, which surprised him. She was a smart, assertive, sweet, friendly woman, just like his mother.

He climbed out of the truck and went around to her door. Though it was open, she was still sitting when he reached her. Taking her hand, he helped her out, then kissed her. He noticed his mother standing in the open doorway and waved to her.

"Why are you so anxious?" he asked.

"I don't know. I love you so much and I want your mom to like me."

"She will," he said, then kissed her once more before he led her toward the house where his mom was waiting.

When they got to his mother, she reached out to hug him, then took Jerilyn's hand.

"Mom, this is Jerilyn. Jerilyn, my mother."

"Mrs. Wilson, so glad to finally meet you."

"Mattie, please." She still held Jerilyn's hand, then took Josh's in her other. Looking from her to him, she said, "I can't say Josh has said much about you, only that he loves you; and that's enough for me. And oh, yes, he's told me you're a teacher too. I know he's eager to get home, but can you come in for a while?"

Glancing at Jerilyn, who gave a silent nod, he said, "Sure, but just a little while."

"How about coffee and chocolate cake?"

Jerilyn told her, "Chocolate cake is my favorite; would be hard to turn it down."

Mattie had already made a fresh pot of coffee. Cups were on the table along with the cake, plates, and forks.

As she filled the cups she asked, "Cream and sugar?"

"No, black for me."

"Me too."

"Seems we all like our coffee the same way."

Josh's mother told her, "I remember seeing you with Josh at Mark and Austen's wedding, thinking what a pretty girl you were. He should have introduced us then."

"I should have," he said. "But I didn't want to share any of my time with her."

"I think I understand. I'm so glad you've found your special lady. Now that she's here for a few days, I hope you'll give me time to really get acquainted with her," she said, smiling at them both.

"I will, Mom." Standing up, he continued, "Now I just want to get on home. Thanks for the cake and coffee."

As they headed out the door, Mattie asked, "Could you come for dinner on Sunday? Maybe Nancy can be here too."

They looked at each other, both smiling, and nodded. "Yes, let us know the details."

As they walked to his truck, Jerilyn told him, "I like your mother."

"I'm glad. And I could tell she likes you too."

~

It was a short drive to his house, and when they pulled into his driveway, she again felt anxiety. Why? She had known she would be staying with him. She wanted to be there, wanted to be close to him.

He unloaded her bags and came to where she stood, set them down, then took her into his arms, sensing her unease.

"What's wrong?"

"Nothing, really. I want to be here with you. I want to be with you always, but I feel like I'm walking in a dream. Maybe this isn't actually happening?"

Kissing her, he told her, "It's real. I'm so glad it's real, and the next several days we'll be planning our forever after, wherever that's going to be."

"And you're beautiful as always but look exhausted. What time did you get up?" he asked.

"Three thirty."

He was still holding her and said, "No wonder. Now, can you walk by yourself, or do you want me to carry you?"

Smiling, she told him, "I'd love for you to carry me, but I can walk."

When they entered the house, she took a quick look around, refreshing her memory of her previous visit. It had been such a short time and now she realized she remembered very little. Was that good or not?

He led her to her room, the same as before, and asked, "Does it seem familiar?"

"I'm sorry, no. I was so aware of you and being in your house, that's all I could think of. I didn't know you. We had only seen each other a couple of times. And we hadn't even kissed. And we still hadn't kissed when I left."

"But, oh, how I wanted to kiss you. I wanted that from the time I first met you," he told her.

Then she spotted the bridal bouquet, still resting on the dresser where she had placed it before leaving. Moving to it, she picked it up and raised it to her face as if to determine whether there was still a scent.

Keeping it in her hand, she turned toward him, saying, "That was such a happy day."

"Yes, and our day will be happy too."

He was still holding her bags, so set them down, and taking the bouquet, put it back where it had been all those months. Reaching for her hands he told her, "Now I think you need to just rest for a while. I'll order something for a late lunch, or supper. Anything special you'd like?"

"No, whatever you want will be fine. And the bed does look very inviting."

He heard the word "want" and thought, *I want to climb into bed with you and hold you as you sleep.*

He closed the door as he exited. She removed her shoes, pulled back the bedspread, then covered herself with it as she lay down. Despite all the thoughts swirling through her head, she fell asleep almost immediately.

~

Since he couldn't stay with her, Josh checked the box on his house for any mail. There was a mailing from the school district which included a calendar for the upcoming school year. He saw that August 27, a few days before Labor Day, was to be the first day for teachers.

He and Jerilyn had yet to talk about a wedding, where and when and who would be moving—something they planned to do during her visit. He hoped it would be this summer; and if they were going to live in Plattsford, these dates would need to be considered. The same would probably be true if they were in Kansas instead. He thought about the certified university program he had considered when he first contemplated becoming a principal. Would that be a requirement in Kansas too?

Also among the papers was a mention of teacher positions available for the coming year. He saw that a fifth-grade teacher was needed at his school and tried to remember if Jerilyn taught that grade. But would it be a good idea for them to be at the same school? Should he share this information with her before permanent plans were made?

He was thinking how much less complicated things would be if they had experienced a normal first meeting, a normal courtship—whatever that might be. But that hadn't been true for their special friends Mark and Austen; nothing about their courtship had been normal. And he doubted if there was any couple happier than they.

Realizing that he couldn't make any decisions yet, or by himself, he set the information aside to look over the rest of his mail.

When he checked the time, he saw that it had been almost an hour since Jerilyn started her nap. Should he wake her up? Truth was, he wanted to have her in his arms again, but just as he started toward the room, she was standing in the doorway, still with sleep in her eyes and her hair feathered around her face. Looking at her, he felt a tug on his heart. How was he so lucky to have found this special love? He said nothing, just moved to her, placed his hands on her face to raise her lips to his, then there was a kiss unlike any they had yet shared, like it was the beginning of forever.

"Sorry I slept so long."

"It's okay, but it was hard for me not to join you. So, are you hungry? Or did that cake fill you up?"

"I'm ready for a meal. What are we going to have?"

"How about chicken?"

"I like chicken."

While Josh was making the call to order two chicken dinners from Eddie's Café, Jerilyn received a call from Austen.

"Hello."

"Hi, are you in Nebraska now?"

"Yes, settled in with Josh. We stopped to see his mom before coming on to his house. I got up early, so by the time we got here, I was exhausted. Just woke up from a nap. Hope I can sleep tonight."

"How was your trip?"

"Nothing out of the ordinary. As I said, we stopped by his mother's, so we have finally officially met. Don't know why, but I was nervous right up to the time she took my hand. We had coffee and chocolate cake."

"Did you happen to notice her wildflower garden? I think you told me once that your mother had one."

"I didn't notice it. Will have to keep that in mind when we're there for Sunday dinner. And yes, my mother loved her garden. It included lots of hostas too. Unfortunately, gardening hasn't been something I've been able to pursue, but maybe I will."

"I'm looking forward to seeing you," Austen told her. "Do you have plans for tomorrow? If not, maybe you can come to TrailWays?"

"I'll ask Josh and let you know. We have yet to discuss plans for anything, except as I said, we are going to his mother's for dinner on Sunday. Maybe I'll meet his sister."

Seventeen

While they were eating, Jerilyn told him of Austen's invitation to go to TW the next day.

"Guess we do need to discuss what we're going to do the next few days. Should work out okay to go there tomorrow. I'll call Mark later to find out what's going on. Maybe there'll be something special we can join in.

"We're going to Mom's on Sunday. Think I'll check with Nancy to see if she'll be there too. If not, we need to make a date so you two can meet. And how about driving to Scottsbluff on Monday to go to the jewelry store?"

Jerilyn had nodded her head at each suggestion until the question about the jewelry store.

He noticed that and said, "But we can go another time if you'd rather. You do still want to marry me, don't you?"

She reached for his hand, squeezed it, and said, "Yes, yes, yes. I don't know why I was surprised at your mentioning the jewelry store." Then with a smile continued, "I certainly can't say it's sudden. Maybe I was expecting more of a lead-up, like a circus ringmaster announcing the next show."

Josh responded, "You mean like"—standing up and taking a dramatic pose—"and on Monday, a trip to Scottsbluff to the jewelry store to select your engagement ring, and our wedding rings!"

There was applause from Jerilyn as he sat back down and asked, "So, do you want to talk about it later?"

"No. Let's do it; I want your ring on my finger," she assured him.

Jerilyn had risen so she could go to him for a kiss. He had turned his chair and pulled her down onto his lap, then told her, "And I want my ring on your finger."

Just as the kiss was beginning, his phone rang. It was Nancy.

"Hello, Josh. Mom told me she met Jerilyn. She also asked if I could join you Sunday. I can. It'll be good for us to be together; and of course, I'm looking forward to meeting Jerilyn too."

"I'm glad you can be there. We don't see each other enough."

"I won't keep you from her any longer; love you."

"Love you too. Bye."

"That was Nancy."

"Good, I wouldn't want to hear you say 'love you' to anyone else—except your mother. Thank you for supper."

"You're most welcome. I slaved over it all day."

"Of course you did."

Both laughing, they cleaned up, then looked around as if wondering what they would do with the rest of the evening.

"I guess I should get in touch with Dad to let him know I got here. Maybe Jack too to see if everything's okay at home."

Just as she was getting ready to text him, her father phoned. "Guess you got to Nebraska okay?"

"Yes, nothing extraordinary about the flight. Drove by to meet Josh's mother. Then took a nap. Guess I got up too early this morning because by the time we got here, I could hardly hold my eyes open."

At a question from him, Jerilyn said, "Yes. We're going there for dinner Sunday, and Josh's sister will be there too. I talked to Austen later, and she told me that Mattie has a wildflower garden like Mom did. I didn't notice; too nervous just being there. But it's something to check out later. How are you?"

"Same as always. You know I don't have a very exciting life."

"That's not necessarily a bad thing," his daughter told him. "And seems to me you keep yourself busy. Thanks again for the ride to the airport this morning."

"You're welcome. Was that just this morning? Seems longer than that."

"Yes, it does. Take care, Dad."

"You too. Love you."

"And I love you. Bye."

When the call with her dad ended, Jerilyn texted her brother Jack.

"I'm settled in Nebraska for now. Have you moved into my house yet? Hope you find everything okay. Thanks for taking care of it for me. Love you."

~

"Okay. All my obligations are taken care of. Now what? Have you checked with Mark yet on what's happening at TrailWays?"

"They're doing something different this year. Going to have a music night tomorrow. Think you heard about last year when the band got so much attention one of the Friday nights? Mark was playing with them and Austen was singing. They're both going to participate, but asked if we would like to go earlier to visit with them and the Pearsons. He even asked if I'd like to play with them too. Have I told you there were times in the past when I did?"

"You haven't, but guess I'm not surprised. Do you sing too?"

"No, how about you?"

"Austen and I used to sing together along with another friend. But that was a long time ago."

"Maybe you can join in too," he suggested.

"It does sound like fun. Maybe I'll ask Austen about it when we get there? What time are you thinking about going?"

"How about early afternoon?"

"Okay. That's one more thing settled. What next?"

"There are a few days ahead of us. Anything special you want to settle now?"

"There is something I've wondered about since you visited me."

"That long ago? Must have really been worrying you."

"Not worrying, really, not distressing either; just puzzling."

"So, what is it?"

"When I told you I was going to take classes needed to become a special ed teacher, you mentioned requirements for principal and that you were going to begin class this month. Then you announced you're not going to do that after all."

She was sitting on the couch and he joined her, taking one of her hands in his.

"Yes, I can see why that would be confusing. My original thought had to do with earning more money if I were going to be a married man. And I do still plan to pursue it. It was Mark who convinced me not to do it now."

"He pointed out that if I were taking classes while you're visiting, I would be gone much of the time; and then more time doing homework. Why would I want to do that when the main reason for your coming was so we could spend time together? Waiting a few months to begin the process won't make that much difference."

"Thank you, Mark."

"Yeah," he agreed as he lay back on the couch, pulling her on top of him. He reached to trace her lips with his thumb, then drew her face to his. They both shifted their bodies, arms around each other, legs tangled together. And finally, the kiss, each wanting to be closer.

Then Josh pulled away, but still holding her and not moving from the couch.

"This is one reason it might have been better for you to stay with Mom."

She snuggled against him, and said, "Maybe."

After one more hug, he rose. "Too early for bed. How about going for a walk? Maybe you'll meet some of the neighbors."

~

As they began their walk, Jerilyn asked, "How long have you lived here?"

He had to think a while before answering. "It was my second year of teaching, lived with Mom the first year. So, it's been seven years."

"Do you own, or pay rent?"

"I own; well, I do have a mortgage. There are times, though, that I think it might be better to rent—then someone else would be responsible for taking care of any problems."

"It's an established neighborhood. All the families who live here are the same as when I moved in. Most have children, but so far, none have been in my class."

Three kids who were playing in the yard two doors down ran over to them when they recognized Mr. Wilson.

Pointing to each, he introduced them to her, "Bobby, James, and Tina Wright. Their dad and mom are Ben and Lindsey." Holding her hand up, he told them, "This is Jerilyn."

"Are you moving in with Josh—er, Mr. Wilson?"

They looked at each other and said, "Maybe."

As they continued with their walk, he named the people who lived in each house. Besides the Wrights, there were the Rileys, Morrises, and Landons. "Larry Brown and his family live on the next street over. He's sort of the unofficial leader of the band."

It had been a long day for her and despite her earlier nap, she was beginning to feel drained, which was not lost on Josh.

"This is probably enough adventure for today. Looks like you need to get home and in bed."

Thinking of what her dad had mentioned a few hours ago, Jerilyn did feel as if the day had been more than twenty-four hours long. Hopefully, she would have a good night's sleep and tomorrow wouldn't be so eventful.

Josh walked her to the door of the room which would be hers for the next couple of weeks. "Wish I didn't have to say good night here."

"Me too."

"Love you," he said, giving her one of the sweet kisses that promised so much.

"Love you, too."

She waited until he turned away before closing the door.

Eighteen

Austen and David greeted them as soon as they drove in at TrailWays, with hugs for both Jerilyn and Josh.

"It's so good to have you here. Mark's on a short trek with a family—their first. Recently he's begun doing a bit extra with first-timers, wanting to make sure they absorb the atmosphere and character of the trail and the pioneers who traveled it in the 1840s."

"That's probably what I will need," Jerilyn told her. "The trek you took Maggie and me on when we were here was cut a little short," glancing at Josh as she said it. "How are you feeling? You certainly have that glow 'they' say pregnant women wear."

Austen replied, "I can't complain, especially after hearing my mother talk about her pregnancies."

"So, are you helping on any of the treks?" Jerilyn asked.

As they moved into the house, Austen answered, "Ha, ha. Mark has laughingly told people that person he hired last year isn't available."

Josh broke into the conversation. "Yeah, he told me that when we had lunch together in the spring."

"Continuing her thought, Austen said, "So far, he's limited what he lets me do, being so protective, but so loving." She went on with, "I am continuing with the stories, but not as part of the treks. So far, they're alternating with the music at the Friday Night Feeds."

Josh asked, "What about David?"

Hearing his name, the little boy told them, "Mark says I'm in'spensible."

"Mark takes him along most of the time, even on the longer, overnight treks," Austen told her. "And David loves being with him, just as he's always done. By now, young as he is, he's almost an expert, though, of course, there are some things that require more strength than he has. Now, let's go on in the house. You can tell me what's happening with you two and all the decisions you have to make. The Pearsons are going to drive down in a little while.

"Josh, did you bring your guitar so you can play with the band tonight?"

"I did," he said, "and Jerilyn told me that you two used to sing together a few years ago; maybe she can join in too?"

Jerilyn said, "I told him it sounds like fun, but I'm not really sure I'm up enough on the latest songs. I suppose it's all 'off the cuff' with no words and music?"

"Surprisingly, many of them are the same ones you and I used to sing. Imagine, they have become 'golden oldies.'"

"Well, okay, then," from Jerilyn, "I'm probably a little rusty, but have to admit I've missed those performances." Looking at how she was dressed, she asked, "Will this do for my appearance? Josh says we can go shopping for some western wear while I'm here. Otherwise, this is it."

Austen told her, "It will be fine. You can see, it's not much different than what I'll be wearing. I do dress a little differently for story time. Did you see the dress I made last year? I wear it part of the time. Have been thinking of making another but haven't bought any fabric yet. Besides, there's not much 'give.' Not sure how it might fit over my baby belly, as David calls it, as the summer progresses."

Turning to David again, Jerilyn asked him how he felt about becoming a big brother. He went to his mother, wrapping his arms around her, then answered with, "There's a baby in Mommie's belly," patting her, then "kissed" the baby.

When the Pearsons arrived, Jerilyn was glad to see them and have the chance to get better acquainted.

Kate told her, "Jerilyn, it's good to see you again. Been a while. I understand congratulations are in order," and, smiling, continued, "Guess that bridal bouquet worked."

"Maybe. It's still resting on the dresser in the room at Josh's. Perhaps I should plan to frame it and keep for always."

Josh added, "Strange as it sounds, having it there helped me through those months when we weren't communicating. I would step into the room remembering when Jerilyn was there, then see it and think maybe there was still a future for us."

He sounded so sad, Jerilyn took his hand, "I'm glad you kept it there." then kissed him.

He told the others, "We're planning to drive to Scottsbluff on Monday to check out rings. Some of her friends thought I should have had one before I proposed."

Mark had just walked in and said, "If you remember, I didn't have a ring when I proposed." He reached Austen, wrapped her in his arms, and gave her one of his kisses that never got old.

Then acknowledging her, said, "Hi, Jerilyn, good to see you again."

She told him, "You, too. I understand you're not letting Austen help with the treks."

"She's still telling her stories. And yes, last year, she proved to be one of the best hands I've ever had. But it's a bit different with her being pregnant. At least, I think so. And David is filling in a lot," he said as David ran to him. It was obvious the two were still great pals.

While Mark showered and changed clothes, Bill Pearson told Josh and Jerilyn that the caterer's wagon would be providing food for the night's event.

"No idea how many people to expect. There was quite a crowd for Friday Night Feed last night. Several seemed interested when the announcement was made about the music night. Maybe they'll come back."

As they waited for Mark, Jerilyn said to Austen, "You haven't said anything, so I'm wondering if you know that my brother and your sister have been going out together?"

"She has mentioned that they see each other occasionally at certain events, but no indication it's more than that," Austen told her. "What's your impression?"

"I can't say how Linda feels, and Jon doesn't actually say much," Jerilyn told her, "but I can tell by the way he talks about her, she's special to him."

"I shouldn't be surprised; she's always been mum about anyone she might be spending time with. And frankly, I don't believe she has dated much; she's particular. Think I'll call

Mom later and see what she knows. And I don't know Jon, but I know you, so I'm sure she couldn't find anyone better," Austen said.

~

Mark was carrying his guitar when he came out of his room. "Okay, everybody, it's time for the caterer to be here, and we need to eat first, so we'll be ready to 'perform.'" Continuing with a grin, "And maybe we should rehearse a bit."

Then, "We might as well each take our own pickups since we'll be going different directions when everything is over."

Some of the band members were waiting for the caterer's wagon to open its serving windows, and seeing him, one said, "Hey, Josh, glad you can join us tonight." Josh was carrying his guitar and holding Jerilyn's hand as they headed in that direction.

"This is my fiancée, Jerilyn Tate," he told them.

The word "fiancée" brought surprised looks. Most of his acquaintances didn't know there was a special someone in his life. Though some had seen him with Anita, or probably more accurately, Anita hovering around Josh.

"She's visiting for a couple of weeks and she's joining us for music night. She and Austen used to sing together when they were younger."

He introduced them, and all said they were glad to meet her, then one asked, "How long have you two been together, and why are you just now introducing us?"

He gave them a brief history of their long-distance courtship, then reminded them they all needed to get their food so they could get a few minutes of practice in before the official beginning of Music on the Trail.

~

All were pleased with the number of people who came for the night, and the band got good reviews. Josh and Jerilyn were happy to have been part of the evening. Someone asked, "Are you two going to join us the rest of the summer?"

They had no firm answer since they still needed to determine their plans for the next two weeks, and for their entire future. But they did tell the band they would be glad to join them anytime they were available.

~

When they got to the parking area, Jerilyn hugged Austen and David and said, "That was fun. Who would have thought we would have a chance to sing together again?"

There was a happy, boyish grin on Josh's face when he agreed it had been a great experience, then wrapped his arms around Jerilyn to give her a kiss which soon deepened. It seemed like forever since he had tasted her lips. Then whistles and applause came from the band, so they drew apart and bowed to their audience.

"Sorry, guys, I forgot you were here," Josh told them while Jerilyn wondered what they thought as she climbed into the pickup.

When Josh got in, he told her, "I hope you weren't embarrassed. I couldn't wait any longer to kiss you."

She told him, "It's okay. I was ready for a kiss too."

On the way to Josh's, they reflected on the evening's events and how each felt about their part in them.

Jerilyn told him, "I actually enjoyed it more than I thought I would, and didn't consider that there might even be applause. That was kind of energizing."

"Yes, it was," Josh said. "I saw some of the kids who have been my students, and their parents in the crowd. Wonder what they thought about my taking part?"

Jerilyn answered with, "They probably felt a sense of 'ownership' since they know you, thinking, 'That's my teacher.' They may even want your autograph."

"If we end up living here, maybe it will become part of our summer schedule."

Going through Jerilyn's mind was, *one more thing to consider in our plans.*

They continued discussing the evening all the way to parking the pickup and heading up the sidewalk to the door. But as soon as the door was unlocked and they moved on into the room, a sense of awkwardness wrapped around them.

"This is only your second night here," Josh said. "How are we going to manage for two weeks?" He returned his guitar to the stand he had left in one corner of the living room, then took Jerilyn's hand and drew her toward the couch. "Let's just sit for a while and talk about tomorrow."

"Okay."

Josh told her, "Church starts at nine o'clock, so we'll need to leave here at eight thirty. Then to Mom's. I'm sure she'll be at church, maybe Nancy too. I'm guessing Mom will have planned to have Sunday dinner and be busy finishing up while the rest of us wait.

"That might give us time to visit with Nancy; or we may just all end up in the kitchen getting in each other's way."

"Then I could get acquainted with both of them," Jerilyn told him.

Nineteen

They garnered lots of attention when they entered the church on Sunday morning. Jerilyn noticed a few people she had seen the evening before who all greeted her with smiles, handshakes, and "Glad to see you again."

Josh looked around to see if his mother was there yet, but saw neither her nor Nancy. But there was Anita sitting near the front. With that, he took hold of Jerilyn's hand and started leading her toward a pew on the opposite side of the worship center. His mother and sister didn't see him when they walked in and headed to the place where Mattie usually sat. Then Josh caught their attention and motioned for them to join him and Jerilyn.

When she reached them, Mattie hugged them both, then introduced Nancy and Jerilyn to each other.

"It's so good to finally meet you," Nancy told her.

"You too," Jerilyn answered.

Mattie started to say she usually sat on the other side and closer to the front, but Josh shook his head. Then she noticed Anita, so went with them to the spot he had chosen. Nancy wasn't there often enough to realize it was a different area than where her mother usually sat.

They missed the looks Anita was sending their way. As she often did, she had planned to sit next to Mattie, always hoping Josh would join his mother, despite having heard and knowing of his love for the girl from Kansas. And now, there she was with him and his family. Since the service hadn't started yet, she chose to leave, exiting by the side door. Glancing up just then, Josh was glad to see her go.

Jerilyn enjoyed the service. The songs were a bit different, but for the most part everything was similar to what she was accustomed to. It would be a place where she could feel comfortable and at home.

The Thomas family was there too, and David ran over to give them hugs and asked, "Are you gonna come home with us?"

Josh told him, "Not today, but maybe we'll come by later in the week."

Mattie had prepared what used to be her family's typical Sunday dinner—not quite the same as might be expected. There was lasagna, broccoli, salad, Texas toast, and chocolate cake for dessert. Since it was summer, there would be iced tea for the beverage, and coffee also for those who might want it. Sometimes the vegetable was different, but it was a meal that could be quickly put together after church, with the lasagna made ahead of time and only needing to be warmed up before serving.

Josh mentioned the day before that Jerilyn and Nancy could spend time getting better acquainted while his mother finished the meal, then said, "But we might all end up helping."

Just as he predicted, the kitchen did become the center of activity, as they all helped to get everything to the table. Working together provided the opportunity for Jerilyn to learn more about Mattie and Nancy, and for them to get better acquainted with her. There was almost a dance as they each moved in and out of each other's way and carried on conversations while making sure they accomplished whatever task they had adopted.

Mother and daughter grinned at each other when they noticed that every time Josh got near Jerilyn, he gave her a kiss. And they couldn't help wondering how soon there would be a wedding, where would it be, and where would the couple end up living.

With so many busy hands, it wasn't long before the food was arranged buffet style, with a stack of plates and silverware at one end and drinks on the table. Before they started serving themselves, Mattie asked Josh to give thanks for the food and all their blessings.

During part of their conversation, Jerilyn mentioned her mother's flower beds and herb garden and told Mattie, "I'm sorry that I didn't pay much attention to them, but they gave her so much pleasure. I see that's also an interest of yours."

"Yes, absolutely," Mattie responded. "Maybe while you're still here, you can come by and see if I have some of the same ones."

"I'd like that," Jerilyn told her. "Who knows, maybe I'll decide to have my own gardens some time," glancing toward Josh as she said it. "But I'll have to learn everything."

~

After the meal and the cleanup, everyone moved to the living room. Josh and Nancy didn't get together very often, so they spent some time catching up. Then she turned to Jerilyn. "So, you have two brothers. Are they older or younger?"

"Yes, Jack and Jon. They're both younger, but ever since they were big enough to do so, have taken it upon themselves to watch out for me. Josh will have to tell you about their actions when he visited over Memorial Day weekend."

"Well mainly, I think they wanted to be sure my intentions were good," he told her. "They were wearing their uniforms when I arrived, hoping to intimidate me."

"Uniforms, huh? Military service or otherwise?"

"Jon is a firefighter, and Jack is a police officer," Jerilyn told her. "My dad wasn't amused."

"It's okay," Josh told her. "I'm glad there are plenty of males around to keep you safe when I'm not there," pulling her toward him for another kiss.

As Josh was relating his meeting with the brothers, Nancy had been looking back and forth between him and Jerilyn, and couldn't help commenting, "Lots of J's." And her brother responded, "Yeah, we kind of figured that out. Her mother was a 'J' too—Joyce—and her father is Jeff."

Mattie kept quiet as long as she could, then blurted out, "So what plans do you have for a wedding? Have you decided who's going to have to move?" Then, thinking she had probably said too much, put her hand over her mouth.

The other three couldn't help laughing. They knew that was on everyone's mind and it might as well have been Mattie who voiced it.

Josh took Jerilyn's hand, then told his mother, "Obviously that is one of the big decisions we'll be discussing these two weeks. She's only been here two days so far," then continued, "We're going to Scottsbluff tomorrow to check out rings."

Jerilyn added, "I've been considering those things ever since we've been officially engaged. And I'm sure Josh has too. But so far, it's only been in our individual minds, maybe because we haven't been ready to face the big changes that have to be made."

Looking at his mother and sister, Josh told them, "I'm open to hearing your thoughts. Whatever we decide—here or there—you'll be affected."

Jerilyn nodded and said, "Seems like we need a nudge from someone. But I do know I want to get married in Overland Park. I hope that won't create a problem for any of you, because I want you all there. Austen and her family too. And maybe even the Pearsons. Though if Mark is gone, they may need to stay here to oversee the TrailWays events. Unless we don't get married until the season is over."

Those last words were said with a sadness in her voice. She didn't want to wait that long, but it was already the end of June.

Nancy said, "Well, these days, destination weddings seem to be a popular occurrence. So, it could be that for us."

"And there are certainly plenty of places one can stay," Jerilyn told them. "So, there'd be no problem on that front."

"Okay," Josh said with a grin, "Seems like we've already got two things checked off the list, and there're still several days ahead of us."

Then Jerilyn said, "I know it's important to set a date. And I do want it to be as soon as we can get everything figured out. But since I've been here, I've been thinking that before anything else, we've got to decide where we're going to live, and which of us will have to change jobs."

Then continued, "When he was driving me to the airport for this trip, Dad did tell me that if I was the one who moved, it would be a new place for him to visit," and squeezed Josh's hand. "It's probably a good thing that you've reminded us. None of that means it's going to be an easy decision. One of us will have to move, leave our job, and get another one. It would be so much simpler if we lived next door to each other."

Seeing her distress, Josh wrapped his arms around her and told her, "I never liked any of the girls who lived next door to me. Though at the ranch, it was more like a mile or two."

Jerilyn couldn't help laughing when she said, "And I didn't like any of the boys who lived next door to me. Guess we're just too particular."

"Nothing wrong with being particular," he said as he drew her closer and kissed her. "But look at it this way, either way, and no matter when, one of us will still have a job; and we'll still have a place to live. Sure, there's the moving, but at least we won't have to catch the next wagon train. So, let's leave this for another day. I'm ready for some chocolate cake and coffee."

~

As they were finishing up their dessert, Jerilyn said, "There is one thing I'd like to pass by both of you," looking at Mattie and Nancy. "I've been thinking that since I plan to get married in Kansas, maybe we could have a reception here. That would allow us to include your friends who can't come to the wedding. But it could mean some extra responsibility for you."

Both of them liked the idea, and Mattie told her, "Oh that would be so wonderful. And I can think of several of my friends who would be glad to help."

They had moved into the living room when Nancy asked, "Besides ordering rings, what else do you have planned for these two weeks?"

Jerilyn was wondering about that too and glanced at Josh with a questioning look.

"Well, I haven't talked to Jerilyn yet," he said. "I was thinking that besides the trip to Scottsbluff, we could take a drive through the countryside so she can get a feel of Nebraska—at least this part of it. We might see some of our 'exotic' animals."

He continued, "And there's the Fourth of July celebration at TrailWays. Maybe we'll even do an overnight on the trail. We did drive by my school when she was here last year. I might check to see if we can go inside so she can see the classrooms."

"Wow, how exciting can you get?" Nancy teased.

Her words made Josh realize he hadn't planned anything special for Jerilyn's visit and now looked at her with a miserable look on his face. Then he said, "Guess I was just so excited knowing you were going to be here where I could see you and be with you every day, and not thinking about anything else."

Jerilyn told him, "It's okay. Don't worry about it. To be honest, if you had been coming to visit me instead, I would have felt the same way and just waited for you to arrive.

"I keep thinking about Austen and Mark and how they wasted a summer, avoiding any intimacy, and not appreciating how special it was to be together."

The conversation had started with them separated, but they had moved closer together, stepping into each other's arms for a warm embrace, then a kiss, bringing smiles to his mother and sister.

Nancy said she needed to get on home and headed toward the door, telling everyone, "Bye." Then to Jerilyn, who was still standing with Josh's arms around her, "I look forward to seeing you again soon. And I'm glad both you and my brother were particular. From what I've seen, you're perfect for each other."

After his sister left, Josh and Jerilyn went back to the kitchen, where Mattie was cleaning up their dessert dishes and loading them into the dishwasher. "This has been such a wonderful day," she told them. Then glancing at the two, said, "I agree with Nancy. I'm just sorry that I may have created a situation that kept you from each other for those several months."

Josh knew what she was speaking of, and Jerilyn had an idea it had something to do with Anita. They both went to her, putting their arms around her for a group hug. "It's okay, Mom. Maybe we needed that extra time, so when we finally did get together, we knew it was right and appreciated it more."

Josh took Jerilyn's hand and told his mother, "You're right, it's been a wonderful day, but I'm ready to head on home. Might even take a nap," he continued, drawing a questioning look from Jerilyn. At which he just grinned and said, "Maybe you'd like a nap too?"

Twenty

Jerilyn glanced at Mattie's flower gardens as they walked toward Josh's pickup. She saw some plants she thought might be wildflowers, a favorite of her mother and of hers too, when she took time to study them. They might not require as much attention as other varieties, and probably attracted butterflies, and maybe even hummingbirds. Then she wondered if there were hummingbirds in Nebraska.

Josh noticed her attention to the flowers and asked, "So which ones do you want to grow?"

She pointed to those she was studying and said, "I'd start with them. I think they're wildflowers, and maybe wouldn't require a lot of work."

"Start? That sounds like you might have in mind to have several beds."

The word "beds" brought other images to mind. Probably a good thing they had reached the truck and climbed in.

"I like your sister," Jerilyn told him, wanting to get a different subject in her head, and his too.

He knew what she was doing and let it pass. "Yeah, she's pretty special. Probably haven't appreciated her enough. She always had plenty of guys hanging around, but don't think

I ever thought about checking them out like your brothers. Guess she must be particular too. Can't remember whether there's ever been anyone special, and if so, what happened," he said, thinking of Mitchell Robbins and wondering how the two might get along.

~

When they walked into Josh's living room, he pointed out his oversized couch and said, "I was serious about taking a nap. Want to take one with me?"

Jerilyn thought to herself, *yes, I would*. But didn't answer him, only giving him a look as if to say, "You can't be serious." But she did say, "I don't think that's a good idea."

"Oh, come on, look how spacious it is." He took hold of her hand and moved to the mentioned piece of furniture. "There's plenty of room and I promise I'll be good, just hold you in my arms and nothing else. I'll keep my hands to myself."

"But I'm not sure I could." She hadn't meant to say the words out loud and blushed when she realized she had.

Still holding her hand, he sat down and pulled her down beside him, then started taking off his boots. "What will you do while I sleep, sit and look at me?"

"Okay."

"Okay? You mean you'll lay down with me?"

"Yes, if you promise to be good."

"I promise, though it won't be easy," he told her as he reached down to remove her shoes and said, "Maybe we'll get you some boots when we're in Scottsbluff."

He made himself comfortable on the couch, then pulled her down beside him, and wrapped his arms around her. He fell asleep almost immediately, surprising Jerilyn.

She laid for a while, relaxing, even nestling against him, musing on this unexpected happening, then she too was soon slumbering.

He woke while she was still asleep, savoring the contentment he felt having her in his arms. How was he so lucky to have met and fallen in love with this special lady, and to have her fall in love with him?

"Thank you, God, for sending her to me."

Josh pulled her closer, the movement disturbing her sleep, but not waking her. Instead, Jerilyn turned, cuddling against him. So, he continued to hold her, moving slightly to get more comfortable, then went back to sleep.

It was several more minutes before Jerilyn woke and Josh opened his eyes about the same time, smiling into hers. "Hi," he said, wanting to kiss her, but realizing she wasn't completely awake, restrained the feeling. He could tell she was just beginning to remember how they had come to be together on his couch, and he didn't want her to regret her decision to join him.

"How long have we been asleep?" were her first words.

"A while. I woke up once but didn't want to interrupt your slumber. Besides, it felt so good having you in my arms, I didn't want to move anyway," he told her.

Then he pulled her closer, if that was possible, not wanting to wait any longer for a kiss and the taste of her lips. They both moved to get more comfortable and just as their lips touched, Jerilyn's phone rang. It was in her purse, but it was on the floor next to the couch, and the ringing was not easy to ignore. Why hadn't she muted it?

Still, thinking it was probably a good thing they were interrupted, she sat up, retrieved the phone, and looked to see who was calling.

"Hi, Dad," she greeted her father. "How are things there?"

"Okay," he told her. "A couple of your friends at church asked about you, wondering what exciting things you might be doing."

If they could see me now, they would know, Jerilyn thought. Josh had risen and was now standing, looking out the front door—at who knew what. "We went to TrailWays last evening and both of us participated in Music on the Trail. It's new for them this year. They're planning to have the event once a month. To church this morning. Josh's mother and sister were there, then we went to his mother's for lunch.

"It was my first meeting with Nancy, so it was a good chance to get acquainted and learn a little about each other. She's a physical therapist and lives in Scottsbluff."

"Anything different with you?"

"No," he said. "You know me, pretty much the same thing every day or every week. Both your brothers were at church this morning. Don't know if they came together, but Jayden was sitting with Jack, and Linda with Jon. We visited for a short time after the service. That sounds kind of strange, since Jon is still living here, but we don't seem to be together often enough to visit. And of course, Jack is at your house.

"Oh yeah, do you remember Sergeant Moore? He's been talking to some of the other retired guys about the possibility of a get-together. Not sure when or where, but it'll be good seeing everyone. It's so easy to lose track of people."

"I do remember him," Jerilyn said. "He was always more outgoing than many of the others. Sounds like a good idea. I'd be interested to know who shows up."

"Don't really have anything else," Jeff said. "Say hi to Josh."

"I will," she told him. "Tell my brothers to be careful."

Jeff assured her he would, then told her, "I love you. Bye."

"Dad says hi," she told Josh.

"Hi, Dad," Josh said.

"Love you, Dad. You take care too. Bye."

Jerilyn walked to Josh, who was still standing at the doorway looking out. Putting his arms around her shoulders, he pulled her close, then leaned down for a kiss.

"What are you looking at?" Jerilyn asked.

"Nothing really," he told her. "Just wondering and thinking, mostly. Unless we get married tomorrow," stealing a glance at her as he said it, "I'll still be here by myself." he finished almost mournfully.

"Anyway, maybe I need to do something to make the yard less blah. You know, more than just green grass," he told her.

Jerilyn answered with, "Well, let's go out and walk around the house." At the same time thinking she might be living there herself in a few months. "We can check with your mother for some suggestions. Though I doubt this is a good time of year to start new plants. They would certainly require extra care. But she might have some things she could give us starts of."

Josh asked, "A start?"

Jerilyn told him, "I remember friends and neighbors and relatives coming to our house and Mom digging up and separating plants to give them starts. They took them home and dug a place for them in their own garden. Mom said her garden was spread into several towns and even different states. Now when those people look at their plants, they have a special memory of her."

When they started looking around the yard, Josh realized he had never thought much about beautification, just being sure to keep the yard mowed. But at least it was neat. "So, what do you think?" he asked Jerilyn.

Flashing a grin at him, Jerilyn answered, "Low maintenance."

Josh laughed and said, "For sure. Besides, if there were other plants and flower beds, they'd probably be full of weeds. What about your yard? I sure didn't give it any notice when I was there. All my attention was on you."

"I have to say, it's about the same as yours. Keep thinking every spring and summer I should do something," she told him. "Especially on days after I have visited Dad and seen all the special plants and flowers Mom used to create a beautiful, restful yard.

"Well, it's something we can decide later," she said. "I'm sure your mom will have some ideas."

When they were back in the house, Jerilyn asked, "What do you usually do on Sunday afternoons?"

"During the school year I'm usually working on school stuff," he told her. But for the last several years, I've spent entire weekends at TrailWays, at least in the summer. Remember the Pony Express Rider? I've also served as Wagon Master at times. Of course, that wasn't just on weekends. It hasn't been unusual to spend every summer day there, even if there aren't any treks."

"What day of the week did you come to visit last year—the beginning of our journey?"

"Maggie and I arrived late on a Tuesday afternoon. You came in from one of your Pony Express rides shortly after we got there," Jerilyn reminded him.

"I remember that," he said as he took her hand, smiling as he recalled that first time he saw her. "Almost forgot there was someone else with you."

He had gladly accepted Kate Pearson's invitation to have supper with all of them, so he could spend a few more minutes with her.

"I told you what I do in the summer," Josh said. "How about you? Cruises, vacations in exotic places?"

"Oh, of course," she laughingly replied. "You know what fabulous incomes we teachers have. There have been a few vacations, mostly going to places within driving distance, like the Ozarks, or to visit relatives we don't see very often."

"Though I must admit, I wouldn't mind a cruise to Cozumel and Grand Cayman. A friend did that recently and told me about it. You can swim with the dolphins, learn how chocolate is made, see the Mayan ruins."

"Back to reality: I have also taught summer school, and helped with Vacation Bible School at church. Coached a girls' softball team once, and there were times that I babysat Maggie's and Austen's kids. I think I mentioned that when we first met," glancing at him when she said it to see if he remembered.

He smiled and nodded, then told her, "You're certainly multi-talented."

Twenty One

As they planned, Monday meant a trip to the jewelry store in Scottsbluff to choose an engagement ring as well as wedding bands. Several trays of rings were brought for their consideration, but they soon learned they had similar preferences and quickly agreed on what they wanted.

When they settled on the engagement ring, Josh took it in his hand, knelt in front of Jerilyn, and asked, "Will you marry me, Jerilyn Tate?"

She teared up and nodded. "Yes."

Josh placed the ring on her finger, then rose to give her a kiss. They continued hugging as she removed the ring, handing it back to Josh, who in turn handed it to the jeweler. Along with one wedding band, it required a slight adjustment, meaning a return trip later in the week. Josh was more upset than Jerilyn. He wanted the ring to stay on her finger.

~

They had made plans with Nancy the day before to have lunch together, and headed toward the building where she worked. It was a bit early, so they parked and went in to wait until she was free. She waved at them when she saw them come in and gestured toward a couple of chairs in a corner as she continued the therapy session with a young man.

When he turned their way, he recognized them and said, "Hi. Imagine seeing you here."

Nancy looked from him to the other two with a questioning look.

Mitchell Robbins explained, "I sat next to your brother both directions when I made my recent trip to KC. Then I met his girlfriend last week when she flew in."

"How did you know he's my brother?" Nancy asked.

"Nosiness, mostly." Mitchell told her. "Just talking. I learned his name and asked if he was related to you."

Nancy wondered why it mattered to him. There was a flirtiness about him that she had tried to ignore, while admitting to herself she liked it.

"Guess your session is over for today," she told him. "They came to take me to lunch."

Mitchell seemed disappointed, but only said, "Okay. Next week, same time, same place?"

Josh asked, "Why don't you come with us?"

He and Nancy both looked at him, then each other, and shrugged their shoulders. That was unexpected. "Really not sure if it's okay for him and me to be together. He's a patient, and I'm his therapist." At the same time thinking she would like to have him come with them.

Then Mitchell said, "We can make this my last session. Only reason I've kept coming has been to see you," he told her.

That was a surprise, but she had noticed he didn't seem to need therapy any longer.

"Okay," she agreed.

"You sure?" Mitchell asked.

When he was convinced she was serious, he asked, "So where are we going?"

After some discussion between the four of them, a place was decided on. Then Mitchell asked Nancy, "Why don't you ride with me?"

The other therapists smiled as they watched them leave. They had all noticed the glances the two stole at each other over the last several weeks, wondering how long it would be before they realized their mutual attraction.

When they got to the parking lot, she was surprised to see the car he led her to. She was expecting a pickup, seemingly the standard vehicle of Nebraska farmers and ranchers. Instead, there sat a sporty black Mustang convertible. Seeing her puzzlement, Mitchell just grinned. "Glad I left the top up, but maybe you'd like to ride with it down next time?"

During their lunch, Nancy kept wondering how she had come to be there with Mitchell by her side. The ride over was mostly silent, with each glancing every so often toward the other. Lately she had found herself looking forward to the therapy sessions with him, and if she was honest with herself, dreading when he no longer needed them. Now the decision had been made that there would be no more, but she was with him. What would happen later? Would she see him again after today?

As for Mitchell, he too had dreaded the last session, even though he knew that should have occurred earlier. What next? At least she agreed to ride with him to the restaurant.

"What exciting things have you two been doing?" he asked Josh and Jerilyn after their food was served.

"Probably the most exciting was picking out our rings," Josh told him.

At those words, Mitchell looked at Jerilyn's hand. She said, "There needed to be some adjustment. We'll have to come back later."

"How long are you going to be here?" he asked her.

"Another week and a half," she answered. "And so far, we seem to just be deciding each day what we're going to do," stealing a glance at Josh as she said it. "And there are still specific decisions we need to make."

"I have an idea," Mitchell said. "How about you come visit the ranch? You, too," he said to Nancy. "I could come pick you up if you give me your address."

Josh and Jerilyn couldn't help smiling at how smoothly he inserted his invitation while asking for Nancy's address.

"And maybe you should give me your phone number too?"

After some discussion, with Nancy still seeming to be in some kind of a daze, plans were made for a visit the next Sunday afternoon. That gave her almost a week to prepare for the unexpected alteration in her life.

On the way home, Josh and Jerilyn talked about how their planned lunch with Nancy changed from what they expected.

But it took care of the question in his mind as to whether he should mention his conversation with Mitchell to her. Seemed that Nancy already had feelings for him.

"What do you think now?" he asked Jerilyn. "Is it a good connection?"

"What a word," she responded. "Connection. Is that what we are?"

He reached for her hand and told her, "Yes, we are a connection, a bond, with a special relationship. And I don't want to be disconnected from you."

"Put that way, it doesn't sound so bad. So, in answer to your question, yes, they seem perfect together to me," she told him. "But I still don't know either of them very well, not even your sister.

"So, I'll ask you, how do you think Nancy will feel about being at the ranch? Was she disappointed when your parents had to sell your ranch?"

Josh was taken aback by the question. He had never considered how she might have felt. "Maybe we'll learn more about that on Sunday," he told her.

Changing the topic of conversation completely, he said, "When our grandparents were young, there were no seat belts, and no bucket seats, so they could snuggle up close to each other, his arm around her as they drove along."

"And he would be driving with one hand?" Jerilyn asked. "Were there lots of accidents?"

Josh answered, "I don't know about accidents. But I'm pretty proficient driving with my left hand. See?," as he grabbed her hand. "But, not too smooth if I have to shift gears," he added as he released it.

As they drove into his driveway, Josh said, "Just remembered I told you we should get you some boots while you're here. Shall we plan to go shopping after we pick up our rings?"

"Sure," Jerilyn answered. "Then I can wear them when we go to the ranch on Sunday."

When they were inside the house, Josh brought up a subject they had ignored so far.

Wrapping her in his arms, he asked, "When are we going to get married? And where are we going to live?"

She put her arms around him to get closer. "Yes, we have to talk about those things, and make decisions. But right now, I just want a kiss. We've hardly kissed all day and I need one to remind me of why I'm here and how much I love you."

Josh picked her up, kissing her as he did so. Keeping his lips on hers, he carried her to the couch where they had napped the day before. With her in his lap, he continued the kiss as he lay down, pulling her on top of him, and asked, "Did that answer your question?" Then he rolled so they would be on their sides, facing each other.

"Almost," she said, then taking his face in her hands, pressed her lips against his once more.

After a while, Josh told her, "Unless you're ready for this to go further, we need to stop."

"I know," Jerilyn said as she sat up. "And I know we need to make decisions. Can we plan to talk about it tomorrow?"

"Promise?" he asked.

"I promise."

Twenty Two

The kiss brought Austen and Mark to her mind. There was no question they were very much in love after a troubled start. It had taken an entire summer for each to accept and admit their love for the other, with only an occasional unexpected, unplanned kiss. Which was probably the reason that now they were often seen stealing quick, sweet kisses as they went through the day.

Jerilyn wanted so much to have a love like that. Why couldn't she be more confident of their love for each other? Was it because of those several months the past fall and winter, and even into early spring, when each thought the other had developed a relationship with someone else?

She heard a sound from Josh and looked his way to see a questioning look on his face.

"Deep thoughts?" he asked. "You seem to be a million miles away."

Not wanting to explain all that was on her mind, if that was possible, anyway, she told him, "I was thinking about Austen and Mark."

"After those kisses?" he asked as he started moving toward her.

She let him reach her, then put her arms around him and rested her head on his shoulder. "I just keep thinking how happy they are, and I want the same for us."

"Me too," he admitted. "I don't ever want you to be uncertain about my love."

They separated, and Josh went to check his mailbox. There was more information from school, and Jerilyn could tell he was debating whether to open it. She noticed the return address and told him, "It's probably important. You should see what it's about."

Josh took the papers out of the envelope, glancing at the contents as he unfolded them. Some were duplicates of the mail he received the day Jerilyn arrived, including more information about the opening for a fifth-grade teacher. Noticing that, Jerilyn took it from him to read over. Might it be an indication that she should plan to be the one to move? She didn't want to insert superstition into the decision. It could even be a sign from God.

"I'll keep this and ponder it," she told Josh.

It had been a busy, eventful day. First selecting their rings, even though they had to be left at the jewelers for adjustment, then lunch with Nancy and Mitchell, who might become a couple. In her mind, Jerilyn even added the arrival of the mail from the school district, since it could also affect her future. But there were also those special moments after she begged for a kiss.

So it surprised her when bedtime came that she was reluctant to go to bed, even though she felt drained. Josh seemed hesitant too, lingering with her at her door, where they shared a deep kiss. He headed toward his room, then turned back for one more.

It was a restless sleep for Jerilyn when she finally got to bed. Josh was so much on her mind and she kept remembering those kisses and the remembering turned into dreams. She was restless, tossing, turning, and even emitting soft moans.

Josh came to her, wanting to soothe her, reaching to touch her arm and hold her hand as he caressed her face. With eyes still closed, Jerilyn reached for him, and being off balance, Josh fell into the bed beside her, his back to her. She wrapped her arms around him and pulled him toward her, wanting him close.

He turned to gather her into his arms, whispering, "Jerilyn."

How she loved hearing her name from his lips. She traced them with her finger, then pulled Josh's face toward her. Jerilyn so wanted another of those kisses that in one way fulfilled the hunger deep within her, yet somehow created a longing for more.

A knock at her door woke her just before their lips touched.

She heard, "Jerilyn, are you okay?"

Josh had quickly pulled on his pants before he headed to her room. When he received no answer, he opened the door and went in. Jerilyn had a confused look on her face. He told her, "I heard you calling my name," by then having reached her bed.

She sat up, took his hand, and told him, "I was dreaming about you."

"Was it a good dream?" he asked as he sat beside her and put his arms around her. Then, "Are you blushing?"

It was dark, so she was sure he couldn't see the redness in her cheeks.

"Maybe."

"Want to tell me about it?"

"No," she told him. "And you need to go."

Josh answered with, "I don't want to."

"And I don't want you to," Jerilyn admitted, pulling herself from his arms. "But you have to."

"I know." He gave her a kiss, then stood and headed toward the door.

"Sweet dreams," he told her.

"You too."

He turned back to tell her, "I don't want to dream about you. I want you next to me."

The next morning, she didn't remember whether there were more dreams. If so, they didn't disturb her sleep, so she felt rested.

~

She sat at the table while Josh prepared breakfast. Though it had been only a few days since she left, Jerilyn wanted to check on how Jack was getting along and texted him.

"How are things at my house? Any problems? We tried on rings. They needed adjusting, will go back tomorrow to pick them up. Going to get some boots too. I can wear them when we visit a ranch on Sunday.

"There'll be a July fourth celebration at TrailWays. I hear it's quite an event. Do you have any plans for that day? How is Jayden? How are Dad and Jon? Love you all, Jerilyn."

Josh set a plate of bacon, scrambled eggs, and toast in front of her, then brought a glass of juice. "Who are you contacting so early in the morning?" he asked.

"Jack," she told him. "Thought I should see if everything's okay at home. And remember, it's an hour later there. This looks good, thanks."

"You are most welcome, beautiful lady. Happy to serve you," he said as he leaned down to give her a kiss.

"What are we going to do today?"

He sat down with his own plate of food and told her, "I think it's time to talk about the future," giving her a sideways glance as he said it. Though it was the principal reason she had come, it almost seemed as if they were doing everything they could to ignore it. Why was that? Mark and Austen had avoided talking about a future together for months, but neither was expecting one.

Now, though Josh and Jerilyn were planning to marry, they were avoiding making decisive plans. Each had assorted scenarios roaming through their minds, and she couldn't help remembering his statement of the night before, wanting her next to him.

Adding to her disquiet was the text she received from her brother.

"Good to hear from you, Sis. We're doing great here. No, Jayden's not staying, but she's here a lot. No problems, not much we would change if it were ours."

"Sounds like you're keeping busy. Any plans yet as to where you and Josh are going to live? I note you're still calling this house 'my house.' Does that denote something?"

"I'll be working on the Fourth. Think Dad nearly always did. He's doing great, had a get-together with the 'old cops.' Jon's okay. We don't see each other very often because of our different shifts."

"Take care, tell Josh hi."

"Everything okay at home?" Josh asked.

Jerilyn told him, "Yes, Jack says hi." Thinking about what her brother had asked about her house, and Josh's earlier statement that they needed to make plans, she glanced around the kitchen. She had surveyed the house since being here, except for Josh's bedroom, imagining how her furniture might fit, or even whether she needed any of it. She liked how Josh's was organized in a comfortable, homey way. People who knew her might even think she had chosen and arranged it herself.

If Jack should want to buy her house, he could probably use the furniture too. He had none since he still lived with their dad. Those thoughts were still stirring in her mind when they were interrupted by a question from Josh.

"Do you think you could get used to Nebraska—even like it?" He continued with, "I know I said I could move to Kansas, and I would, if that's what I need to do to be with you.

"But I do still want to pursue being a principal, and it would probably happen sooner here because of my history. And we're not sure how easy it would be for me to get a teacher position in Kansas," he said, holding the school mailings, including the ones Jerilyn had taken as he finished those thoughts.

They hadn't finished their breakfast, but she stood, walked to where he sat, took the papers out of his hands, and made a place for herself in his lap, then told him, "So far, I like Nebraska, though I haven't been here long, and really haven't seen much of it. Unless you count that trip Maggie and I took last year to get here. I like your house, and I love you," leaning over to give him a kiss at those last words. "And I saw enough of those papers," she added, pointing toward them, "to know there is at least one opening somewhere for a fifth-grade teacher.

"Besides, I think my brother wants my house, so I won't even have a home in Overland Park."

He was surprised with her moves more than her words, and gathered her closer in his arms for a deeper kiss.

~

Their breakfast was no longer warm when they finally settled down to finish it, but they didn't mind. Important thoughts which had been suppressed were now voiced and ready to be addressed.

Josh told her, "I'm going to call the school offices to see if they're open, and if not, when they might be. I want to get started on whatever needs to be done for you to transfer to a school here. How would you feel about teaching at the same school I do? I don't believe there would be a problem from the district's viewpoint."

He learned that it would be the next week before they could meet with anyone—the day after the Fourth, and the day before she would be returning to Kansas. He made a note of it on the calendar hanging on the wall. Hopefully, they would be able to accomplish what they needed to that one day, but there might still be some long-distance preparation.

After the call, Josh said, "I've got to get some groceries," then checked through the refrigerator and cabinets for a better idea of what needed to be replenished. He asked Jerilyn, "How about you make a list of some things you like?"

Before doing so, Jerilyn too checked his supplies, wondering if his were different than hers. She was also remembering that when he had been with her over Memorial Day, her cupboards were empty.

"Why don't we just wait until we get to the store," she asked, "and check what's on the shelves? If I'm going to be here, I need to get familiar with the store and its layout anyway. And if we're together, we can learn each other's preferences."

"Sounds good to me," Josh answered. "I'll call Mom to see if there's anything she needs and save her a trip."

Mattie told him, "Yes, I do need a few things, but I enjoy seeing everyone at the store. It's a big part of my social life. In fact, I'm ready to head out the door now. Maybe I'll see you there; when are you going?"

"Just a sec, I'll check with Jerilyn."

She told him, "Now would be okay."

He passed that information along to his mother and said, "Guess we'll see you soon."

~

When they saw Mattie, she asked, "Did you get your rings?" checking Jerilyn's left hand.

Jerilyn told her, "We chose them, but a couple needed a little adjustment. We're going back to pick them up tomorrow."

"And she will finally have my ring on her finger," Josh added, reaching for Jerilyn's hand and bringing it to his lips for a kiss.

Mattie wrapped her arms around them with a hug, "I'm so happy for you. What other plans do you have for the time Jerilyn is here?"

Not sure how much to tell her about Mitchell and Nancy, Josh mentioned that they were going to visit a ranch on Sunday afternoon. He was somewhat surprised when Mattie said, "Oh yes, Nancy told me about it. Said it belonged to one of her therapy patients."

"Did she tell you anything else?" Josh asked.

She smiled and said, "Enough."

While driving back to Plattsford after picking up their rings and getting the promised boots, Jerilyn was reminded of the time when Josh took her on a tour of Scottsbluff the day she arrived for Austen and Mark's wedding. She was feeling awkward, tense, and uncertain, thinking about the hours and days she would be staying with a man she was barely acquainted with and certainly couldn't say she knew.

Because of those thoughts swirling through her mind, she hadn't absorbed anything, and remembered none of it. She couldn't say whether they drove past any of the places they had visited recently—the jewelry store, the western store where she got her boots, or the clinic where Nancy worked.

Now, with her left hand held in front of her, she was admiring her engagement ring when Josh voiced a question.

"Can you drive a standard shift?"

Jerilyn was startled at the question, but answered with her own. "No, why? Does it matter?"

"It might. This is a standard," he said, gesturing around the cab. "I think it would be good for you to know how to drive it. We should plan some lessons while you're here, maybe on the way to Mitchell's ranch on Sunday. What do you think?"

She didn't know what to think. She remembered hearing her grandmother tell the story about her brothers trying to teach her how to drive a pickup—the only vehicle the family owned. They really didn't have the patience to teach, and she probably didn't have the patience to learn. After almost driving into a ditch, the lesson ended. Several years later a boyfriend taught her.

"So you not only want me to learn to drive a standard shift, but a pickup at that?" Jerilyn asked. "Remember how small my car is? This is much bigger. It might as well be a tank."

"It's a few more days. I'll let you meditate on it."

Twenty Three

Church services were held at TrailWays one Sunday each month in the summer, and there was one the day Josh and Jerilyn were to visit the ranch. The outdoor service took place in the same covered area where Music Night had occurred, and quite a crowd had already assembled when they arrived. Some of those present recognized Jerilyn from the week before and made a special point of greeting her.

"It's so good to see you again. Are you here for the rest of the summer?" someone asked.

"This will be my last Sunday for a while," she said. Then, holding up her hand so they could see her ring, she added, "But that will change."

"Oh, wonderful, congratulations! So glad for you and Josh. You've probably guessed, he's pretty special to us."

Jerilyn looked around to see who else might be there. She didn't see Josh's mother, and wondered whether she usually attended the TrailWays' services. But there was Anita, who seemed to have noticed when she displayed her ring. She recalled words from her father, "Happy thoughts, Jerilyn, happy thoughts." But it wasn't always easy.

After services, she found Austen to show her the ring. David was interested too and wondered why it was so special. Austen told him, "Jerilyn and Josh are going to be married, like Daddy Mark and I are."

Seeing the questioning look from Jerilyn, she said, "He knows about the expected baby and that I'll be Mommie and Mark will be Daddy. He wants Mark to be his daddy too. We've been in touch with the Wileys to let them know we're starting adoption proceedings. David will have a hyphenated name: Wiley-Thomas."

~

Mitchell had texted Josh at the end of the week to let him know there would be lunch at the ranch. So they were able to head that way with no more delay after stopping to greet all the people who wanted to know about their plans for a wedding.

When they were on the road driving toward the ranch west of Scottsbluff, she told Josh how much she enjoyed the outdoor service. "It was so calm and peaceful. I felt wrapped in a blanket of serenity. Do you ever help provide the music?" she asked. "I noticed those who were there today also played at Music Night."

"Sometimes," he said. "And occasionally at 'regular' church too. It's a special ministry that satisfies a kind of hunger."

"I understand that," Jerilyn admitted. "That's the way I felt when I served on our worship team. I didn't see your mother. Did I just miss her somehow?"

"No, she rarely attends the outdoor services. The congregations in Plattsford take turns providing them. I believe she goes to the other church in town when our congregation is at TrailWays," Josh said. "Maybe I should ask her."

Looking out her window, she made note of the wildflowers growing beside the road, thinking she needed to learn their names. She might want to get some for her own garden next summer. There was a daisy-like one, yellow flowers with a red center, a deep pink one reminding her of phlox, and spiderwort, which she did know. It was a magnet for butterflies. As they drove along, she thought, *I've probably seen more of the Nebraska countryside than that of Kansas, where I've lived all my life.* She and her family didn't get out of the city often.

Mitchell had driven into Scottsbluff to pick up Nancy instead of having her drive. His reasoning was perhaps more selfish than just saving her the trip, as it would give him more time alone with her. When Josh and Jerilyn saw them together, they could tell the two were still getting acquainted, but it was easy to see it was already something more than therapist and patient.

Mitchell's parents, Dennis and Meg, were happy to meet Nancy. Now they understood why their son had continued to go to therapy when they were sure he no longer needed to.

"Josh, we understand Mitchell first met you when you were flying to Overland Park, and then learned you're the brother of his therapist." Looking toward Nancy, they told him, "We like her."

"So, what about you and Jerilyn? How did you two happen to meet, with you in Nebraska and her in Kansas?"

"Do you know about TrailWays?" he asked. When they nodded, he continued, "She's a friend of Austen, and when she came to visit last summer we met. There have been times when things haven't gone well. And there have been misunderstandings. We've both made journeys so we could have actual time together. But now, we're engaged."

It was easy for the Robbins to see his love for Jerilyn. He hadn't taken his eyes off her while he was relating their story.

~

After lunch, Mitchell and Josh saddled horses for the two young couples, it being the most logical way to take the tour. Mitchell rode regularly, since it was his occupation. Josh rode often with TrailWays, and he and Nancy had grown up on a ranch—though Nancy hadn't ridden regularly for quite some time. Each quickly climbed into the saddle, then noticed Jerilyn still standing beside her horse. Looking at Josh, she told him, "The only time I've been on a horse was the day I rode with you back to TrailWays' headquarters."

He dismounted and said, "I'm so sorry, sure wasn't thinking. Forgot that not everyone grows up with horses. Do you want to ride with me, or—?"

"I need to learn to ride. I want to learn to ride," she said. "But some instruction would be useful, as it's obvious I'm not even sure how to get on."

Josh wrapped his arms around her, gave a quick kiss, then helped her mount. "Want to practice?" he asked.

"No, I think I can remember. I just need you to be patient and gentle with me in case I'm a slow learner about everything else."

He had climbed back onto his horse and guided it close to her. "This is a good day for a first lesson. We'll be riding slowly through the fields, not racing around a track, or even chasing a calf to rope."

After some simple instructions, she told them all, "I think I can do this."

As Josh said, the circumstances were almost ideal for a novice rider. Occasionally they dismounted and walked around. She was glad for her boots, and grateful they didn't need to be broken in.

~

On the way home, Josh said, "You sure caught onto horseback riding, but we haven't gotten any driving lessons in. Guess there will be plenty of time after we're married."

Jerilyn heard the 'after we're married' and thought, *It's the first time either of us has used that phrase.*

~

She wore her boots again for the Fourth of July celebration at TrailWays mid-week. She and Josh went to his mother's, then drove her car to the event.

Traditions begun years ago attracted neighbors, people from town, and even as far away as Scottsbluff. Red, white, and blue decorations were wrapped around all the buildings, including the covered stand where Friday Night Feeds, church services, and other regular events took place. Even the horses, mules, and wagons were festooned with the colors. A business in town catered the food, and a band was playing patriotic music. Special games and activities were planned for all ages, and there would be fireworks when it was dark enough.

Jerilyn asked Josh and Mattie, "Is this something you do every year?"

Josh nodded, and Mattie told her, "Way back when, Plattsford had its own celebration, but it couldn't compete with the one here. Now I think people from town even help with this one."

Just as she finished speaking, Nancy walked up with Mitchell and brought him to where her mother stood. "Mom, this is Mitchell Robbins. Mitchell, my mother."

"I'm so glad to meet you, Mrs. Wilson," he said, holding out his hand.

Taking it into hers, she said, "Mattie, please. And I'm happy to meet you." She couldn't help noticing the glow on her daughter's face, and thought, *I do hope this will grow into a happy, permanent relationship.*

The group strolled around, investigating all the activities and checking on the food being served. Mitchell told them, "I've been to TrailWays before, but this is my first July Fourth celebration. Quite an event. I can see why it's so popular."

Though he was relieved of his usual responsibilities on the special days, Mark still moved around among all the visitors, making sure everything was running smoothly. Austen and David were with him when he ran into Mattie and the two young couples.

Overhearing Mitchell's remark, he introduced himself. "It's always good to hear positive comments. I'm Mark Thomas, owner of TW. This is my wife Austen and son David."

Josh said, "Meet Mitchell Robbins. He has a ranch west of Scottsbluff. Raises calves for the rodeo, and sometimes participates."

Mitchell included them all in his comment. "I think it's time to give up the participating and concentrate on the raising. Just as soon not need therapy again. Although without it, I wouldn't have met Nancy." He smiled as he raised her hand to his lips.

The group of five went to the caterer's wagon to get something to eat, then found a place to sit where they could also enjoy the music. Later they checked out the games, where Josh and Mitchell decided to try their hand at pitching horseshoes while the women cheered them on. Jerilyn and Nancy declined to play themselves, but said, "Maybe next year."

They stayed until after the fireworks display, joining in all the oohs and aahs, then headed to the parking area with the crowd of visitors.

As they walked along, Mitchell observed, "That was great. It's been a few years since I attended any Fourth of July events, but Chimney Rock sure provided a dramatic background for the fireworks."

The group reached Mrs. Wilson's vehicle first. Hugs and handshakes were exchanged, and Nancy said goodbye to her mother and brother, then hugged Jerilyn again. "Hope you have a good trip home. I'll see you in about a month. Do you have my number so you can text or call?"

Jerilyn was tearful and could only nod as she returned Nancy's hug.

It had been a happy, exciting celebration day, and the next to last one that Jerilyn would be with Josh before returning to Kansas. So, after driving Mattie home, transferring to his pickup, then traveling the short distance to Josh's, she was feeling sorrowful, depressed, and drained.

~

The next day would be taken up with a trip to the school district offices. There might be forms to fill out, and who knew what else. A busy business day. Would there be even a touch or hint of joy? Jerilyn hoped so; she didn't want her last day with Josh to be ordinary and dull.

It had been quiet ever since Jerilyn's bags were placed in the pickup. She left her boots at the end of the bed, then walked through the house, knowing she would be back in a month.

She wished she didn't have to leave, wondering why they hadn't gone ahead with a very simple wedding at Josh's church, or maybe even at TrailWays. But they didn't, so there they were on their way to the airport at Scottsbluff for her return to Kansas. Josh reached for her hand as soon as they backed out of his driveway, but there had been no words from either. They could see tears in each other's eyes.

Josh told her, "Wish it could be like our grandparents' time, and I could have my arm around you."

To which she answered, "Me too."

~

As they moved nearer to the city, Jerilyn thought of the day before. She was able to get things started regarding teaching in Nebraska, filing the paperwork and paying the fee to get the license, since it would be in a different state. The superintendent they met with mentioned some openings she could possibly fill, even one for a special ed teacher, so she could consider whether she wanted to move in that direction.

Josh had even brought up his wish to be a principal and received some positive feedback. Hopefully, that could happen soon. He knew he would need to complete a certified university program in administration, and believing earlier in the year that he would start the process in the summer, had already filled out forms that were ready to send.

It was quiet as the miles passed. When they got to the airport, Josh dropped Jerilyn off at the curb with her bags, kissed her, and said, "Wait for me." Practically the first words either of them had uttered since climbing into his pickup.

He was able to find a parking spot pretty quickly, all the time thinking, *I'll have to drive home by myself to an empty house. Not sure I'll be able to bear the next few weeks.*

He recalled that first time he had taken her back to the airport to fly home after Mark and Austen's wedding. He didn't know then how important she would become to his life. There wasn't even a kiss, but the time with her had been a sweet beginning. Now it was reaching the end of that foundation and moving to a commencement of the most important one. There had been unexpected disruptions and disconnections after that beginning, resulting in several months of despondency and sadness for them.

"Please, God, let there be nothing more to interrupt our journey," he prayed as he reached her side.

He took the bag she was holding and placed it beside the other, then gathered her into his arms.

"I love you so much; it hasn't been enough time. Wish you didn't have to go. I don't want you to go," he said against her lips. "It will seem like an eternity before our wedding."

"And to me too," Jerilyn told him. "Why didn't we plan differently? But now it's time, and I have to go to finalize plans, but I wish we could be together. What are you going to do the next few weeks?"

"Mark's going to let me help at TrailWays. That's always a good way to pass the time. And I think I'll visit my mother more, never thought before how lonely she must get."

Jerilyn said, "And I'll probably spend some extra time with my dad. I know he's already planning visits to Nebraska, but I will miss him. My brothers have been there, but I realize now, I should have stopped by more often.

"And there'll be completing wedding plans. What about attendants? Since Mark can't come, are you going to have a best man?"

"I hadn't thought about it, what about you? Austen can't come either."

Her flight was announced, which ended their speculation. He took one bag, she the other. They entered the terminal, holding hands, and moved toward the gate, then stopped when they had gone as far as Josh could accompany her.

"Don't forget the rings," she told him. I'll call when I get home. Take care of yourself."

There was one more hug and kiss, each telling the other, "I love you."

Twenty Four

When Jerilyn was flying toward Kansas, and Josh in his pickup driving toward home, each of their thoughts was on the other. There were still plans to be made, too many plans still to be made after two weeks together. But hopefully that would keep them busy enough that the time would pass quickly.

Jerilyn was still sad when the plane landed, thankful she had asked her dad to provide transportation to and from the airport. It was good to see him waiting in the terminal. It was mid-afternoon, but he asked if she would like to have a meal with him before heading on to her house.

Grateful for the invitation, she told him, "Yes, I would. I'm not ready to go home yet. Though I guess it won't be empty because Jack may be there. What about Jon?"

"Not sure," her dad said. "When he's not on duty, he's often with Linda. He sleeps at home, and that's about it."

Jerilyn was jealous thinking of her brothers at that moment, though she was glad they had both found someone who might become their special other. Did they have any clue how lucky they were that their ladies were here in the city where they all lived? She thought back to the day when she and Josh discussed how it might have been better, or simpler at least, if they had fallen in love with the boy or girl next door. But now, knowing how much they loved each other, they were glad that hadn't happened, despite the difficulties of their frequent separations.

On the way to his house, Jeff asked, "Did you two get everything planned?"

"No."

He turned his head to give her a quick glance. Only one word, but it said so much—what, and how much, did it mean?

"Okay," her dad said, "You didn't show me your ring, but I saw it on your finger, so I would guess you're still planning to have a wedding?"

"Yes." Jerilyn told him. When he glanced at her once more, she continued, "Except for getting the rings, it seemed to be beyond our ability to settle on discussing the specifics. Which means that even after being together for two weeks, the rest of the planning is still to be done, and still long distance."

Then she asked Jeff, "Were you able to check available dates at the church?"

"I did," he told her. But without your input, we couldn't very well settle on one. Maybe that's the first thing you need to do, then go from there with the rest of the details?"

They reached Jeff's home, and he was pulling into the driveway with those last words.

As she climbed out of the car, Jerilyn said, "Yes," then smiled. "Maybe that will be enough motivation to get me focused on the rest."

While Jeff got a meal together, Jerilyn called Josh, with fingers crossed that he would answer. There was little conversation that morning, each too sad because of her leaving.

When he answered, Josh asked, "Are you home?"

"Actually, I'm at Dad's," she told him. "Wasn't ready to go home yet. Jack's there, but you're not; it will feel empty to me."

Josh replied with, "How well I know. Once again, I'm asking, why haven't we planned differently? One could almost believe we enjoy these journeys."

"Speaking of planning," Jerilyn said, "I need to check first about a date for the wedding and see if the church is available. How about the second Saturday in August? Will that work for you? We really need to have that settled before we can plan everything else."

"I'll check my calendar," he told her. "But I'm fairly sure that will be okay. Are we going to have a honeymoon?"

Just then, Jeff let her know the meal was ready, and she told Josh, "That's something you can think about. Since you asked, you must have ideas. Dad's got our meal ready, so call me later. I love you."

"Love you too," Josh answered.

They served themselves, then sat at the table. Jeff said grace: "Thank you, God, for the food, and be with Jerilyn and Josh as they finalize plans for their wedding and their life together."

"Thanks, Dad."

He asked, "Putting wedding plans aside for now, how was your Nebraska visit?"

Jerilyn told him, "It was great. Of course, Josh and I got used to being together." At a look from her dad, she said, "Not like that—we were in separate rooms. In fact, I barely looked into his room. So that will be new when I'm Mrs. Wilson."

She pondered that title for a while, the first time she had said it out loud. Had she even thought it? Jeff gave her a few more moments of repose before more questions.

"What about Josh's mother? Did you two hit it off, as they say?"

"Yes," Jerilyn told him. "She's completely different from Mom, except for her flower gardens. It's too late to start anything this year, but she'll help me make some of my own in the spring. Josh's yard is just green grass, so there are lots of possibilities. I might even create a 'Joyce's Garden' in honor of Mom, and include some flowers that were her favorites."

"And his sister?"

"Nancy is quiet, but then thinking about it, guess Josh is too. She's nice, I like her, and think we'll be happy sisters. Did I tell you about the guy Josh met on the plane who happened to be one of her therapy patients? His name is Mitchell Robbins, and he had developed quite a crush—or liking—for her. He has a ranch with his parents west of Scottsbluff. We went there one day. He picked up Nancy, so she was there too."

"And does she like him?" Jeff asked.

"No doubt about that," his daughter said. "But I believe she was surprised at his interest, or maybe just not prepared for it since he was her patient.

"I did get to spend time with Austen at TrailWays. She and Mark are so happy. I want Josh and me to have that kind of love. He's going to be helping some there the next few weeks, so he won't always be available to talk or text. Which means I'll have to make most of the decisions about the wedding without his input. But that may be normal?" with a question at the end and a glance at her dad.

"Well, I sure didn't help much as I remember," Jeff told her. "But that was quite a few years ago, and she did have her mother. Maybe things have changed."

Sadness washed across Jerilyn's face at the reminder she didn't have her mother to guide her as she proceeded with her wedding plans.

"Maybe it would be good to start with a list," her dad told her. "I might be able to help with that, just remembering all the weddings I've attended and things I noticed. But there are your friends Maggie and Lainie, and even Jayden. Bet they would be glad to help. Put that on your list," he said with a grin.

"Okay," Jerilyn said.

1. Date—calendar at church—pastor
2. Get in touch with Maggie for help.
3. Wedding gown—Mom's

"Thanks, Dad. Such a simple, logical thing. Don't know why it hadn't occurred to me. Did Mom have a list? Do you remember?"

"Somewhere in the back of my mind, there's a vague memory that she did."

"Now I think I'm ready to go home."

When they got to her house, Jerilyn commented, "Seems like forever since I was here."

Jeff set down the bags he carried in and gave her a hug. "Love you, Jerilyn."

"I love you too, Dad. I'll call you about Mom's gown. If I'm thinking about wearing it, I should check on it right away in case it needs altering."

Jack wasn't home, but as Jerilyn carried her bags to her bedroom, she could almost feel his presence. He had been there for only two weeks, and she could see no obvious changes. If there were any, they were so subtle she couldn't recognize them, making her wonder if there was any sign of her, her essence in Josh's house. Could he feel it?

She was tired; it had been a long day, but wanting to have at least one thing settled about her marriage, she called the church to determine if the date she and Josh had discussed was available. The offices were closed, so she left a message. Though it was the weekend, she hoped to hear from someone soon. And not wanting to wait any longer, she even went so far as to write "Wedding Day" on her calendar.

With that first item on her list settled, at least in her mind, she was ready for bed a bit earlier than usual.

Since she went to bed early, Jerilyn woke early. Too soon to call anyone, maybe she could send a text, thinking about getting in touch with Maggie. But breakfast first.

Jack was sitting at the table when she walked into the kitchen, his back to her. Momentarily startled, she exclaimed, "Oh!"

He turned around, saying, "Good morning, Sis. Did you forget I was living here?"

"Yes," she told him, "for just a minute." Then walked to where he was by then standing to give him a hug.

Looking at his plate, Jerilyn asked, "What are we having for breakfast?"

"I'm having toast and coffee," he told her. "Don't know about you."

She couldn't help laughing as she recalled those weeks, or was it months ago, when she told Josh that's what she often had for breakfast.

Remembering that, she wanted to hear Josh's voice. Since there was an hour's difference in time, he might not yet have left for TrailWays.

He answered sleepily, "Morning, Love."

Those words made her heart leap; how she wanted to be with him to hear them every morning. But a month's time stretched in front of them.

"Good morning to you, too," she told him. "Don't really have anything to say, except I love you. I'm going to check with Maggie later to see if she can help with the wedding plans, then may go to Dad's to get my mom's wedding gown. I haven't seen it since I was a little girl, when I told her I wanted to wear it for my wedding."

"Will you be at TrailWays today?"

"Yeah, as Pony Express Rider, think you met him once," Josh said.

Jerilyn told him, "Yes, and I fell in love with him, though it took a while for me to realize it. I'll let you go so you can get ready. Call me when you can. Love you."

"You too," he told her. "Bye."

She made toast and poured a cup of coffee for herself, then carried them to the table and asked Jack, "Are you working today?"

"No, it's my day off," he told her. "Jayden and I are thinking about going to Union Station. Since you're home, do you want me to move back to Dad's?"

"Not today. We will have to talk about it sometime, since I'm going to be here, but only for a month," she answered. "It might even be helpful having you around."

Her brother asked, "So you're moving to Nebraska? When's the wedding?"

"Hopefully the second Saturday in August," Jerilyn told him.

"That soon, huh?"

"No, that long," she told him almost sorrowfully. "But there's a lot to be done. And besides the wedding, there's my job to take care of—both here and there. Guess I better notify school here first thing Monday. Hopefully, I'll hear about a position in Plattsford. At least Josh has his job, so we'll have an income regardless of what happens for me."

Then, changing the subject, she asked, "How are you and Jayden doing?"

"I like her a lot, pretty sure she feels the same about me," Jack told her. "But there's some guy who keeps calling her. Which reminds me, I saw that Derek guy at the pool a couple of weeks ago. He asked about you."

"What did you tell him?"

"That you were in Nebraska. It was the day after you flew out."

"And?" she prompted.

Jack told her, "He wanted to know why. I told him you were visiting friends."

"You knew it was more than that," his sister reminded him.

"Yeah, I just wanted to lead him on. He sure seems a bit dense for a teacher. He did ask what friends. I told him Austen, Mark, and Josh. He remembered the names Mark and Austen, and asked if Josh was their son. I just said no.

"Jayden was there and told him Josh was their friend. That seemed to really confuse him. We left so he couldn't question us anymore.

"I thought your friends at school told him you had a love in Nebraska?"

Jerilyn answered, "Well, as you stated, he is a bit dense."

Twenty Five

When Josh arrived at TrailWays, he learned there were two groups on the trails. One was a family with two preteen girls who were there for an overnight trek. The girls told Mark and Austen they had studied about the Oregon Trail and were excited, hoping they would encounter some of what those earlier travelers did.

They lived in eastern Nebraska, so this was their first time to see Chimney Rock. They were told the Pony Express Rider would be stopping by for any mail they might want to send, and deciding to take on the personae of those pioneers, the girls carefully wrote letters describing their experiences since leaving home. The letters would be mailed to themselves and would be there when the girls returned. When Josh rode up, the letters were ready. But first the girls wanted a picture of themselves with him, wishing they had some clothes appropriate to the 1840s.

Austen told Josh those in the other group who were on a two-hour trek consisted of four teachers from Plattsford. "Maybe you'll know them." When he reached the group, he dismounted, as was his usual procedure. His heart dropped as he turned toward the group and realized Anita was one of the four.

She wasted no time in coming toward him and taking his arm. "You girls remember Josh—er, Mr. Wilson, don't you?"

The others were watching closely, wondering at her actions. They did know him, but Anita was acting as if there were something special between them which they knew nothing about.

Still holding onto his arm, Anita said, "I thought you were engaged. What happened? Did she decide she didn't like Nebraska?"

Freeing himself from her grasp, he told her, "I am still engaged. We're getting married in a few weeks, then she's coming back here. She's even checked on possible positions in the school district. Now, if any of you have letters you want mailed, I'll take them."

He climbed back onto his horse, then looked at each of them. But they were all staring at Anita, who had a befuddled look on her face. She had heard that Josh was working for TrailWays, and assumed it meant that he and that Kansas Woman had broken up and decided she would try once again to gain his attention.

The hand who was serving as wagon master noted the exchange between Josh and Anita. He was hired only for the season, so held no knowledge of any previous relationship or non-relationship between the two.

Josh waited a bit longer and when there was no response from any of the teachers, he headed for TrailWays' headquarters. He delivered the letters from the young girls, then went looking for Austen.

She was contrite after hearing about his experience. "I'm so sorry, I didn't know Anita would be with the group. One of the others made the arrangements. And I even heard that Anita resigned her position."

"It's okay," Josh told her. "I figured you didn't know, or you would have warned me."

"Now I need to hear Jerilyn's voice," he said as he headed toward his pickup, where his phone was.

But there was more frustration as his call went to voice mail. The only message he left was, "I miss you so much. Call as soon as you can. I love you."

~

The wedding date was confirmed at church, but there were many other details to consider. There was hardly enough time to send invitations, but if they were to be sent, Jerilyn needed a list from Josh. Then, thinking of lists, she remembered her dad's advice, so she sat down to make one that included all the things she needed to consider, but first she called Maggie to see if she could help.

One item on the list was "attendants" with a question mark. Austen would have been her preference for maid of honor, but she couldn't come for the wedding. And who would Josh want? She also learned that one of them would need to appear in person to apply for the wedding license, which needed to be signed by both parties. She didn't know whether their full names would be necessary, but as his wife, she would like to know it. And Josh had asked about a honeymoon.

With those questions and more, Jerilyn needed to get in touch with him. And she didn't want to send a text; she wanted to hear his voice, which meant she was upset when she heard the message he had left. Why did she set the phone down and leave the room? He was driving when she called him, so as he did, she left a message for him. "I want to hear your voice too; wish you were here, or I was there. I need you."

While she waited to hear back from Josh, Jerilyn wrote a letter of resignation to her school and checked over the application she had completed for a position in Plattsford. She would mail them the next day on her way to pick up her mother's wedding gown at her dad's.

As long as she was completing paperwork, Jerilyn thought she should make her list of people to invite. Maggie had given her some ideas about places for a reception and offered to contact them about availability, and was also going to determine if Ron's Band could provide the music.

Jerilyn was so happy to hear Josh's voice. When he called, she teared up.

He asked, "Is everything okay?"

"No," she told him. "I feel overwhelmed, even though Maggie is helping. I feel like I'm in another dimension without you."

"Do you want me to come?" he asked her.

Jerilyn replied, "How soon can you get here?"

"I did commit to Mark to help the rest of the week." Josh said, "I'll check—"

She interrupted and said, "I'll be okay. Just call me every day. But there are things I need from you, a list for invitations as soon as possible.

"You mentioned a honeymoon. Will we even have time?"

"We'll have time," Josh told her. "Leave that to me."

"Okay," Jerilyn agreed. "You can tell me about it later. Now I need your full name for the marriage license, and we both have to sign it."

"Are you ready for this?" Josh asked. "My middle name is Samuel. How do you like that? Joshua Samuel Wilson."

Hearing that, Jerilyn began to laugh, and he asked, "Is it that funny?"

"No, I'm Jerilyn Sarah, so when we're married, we'll have the same initials," she explained.

"I think I like that," Josh told her. I'll check with Mom right away to get a list together for invitations. But I don't know about attendants. I would ask Mark, but he can't come."

"And I would have asked Austen, and she can't come," Jerilyn added.

"Maybe we can have our parents," Josh opined.

"That's a thought," Jerilyn said. "Not usual, but at least we know they will be there. Let's talk about it later."

"How about I come a week before the wedding?" Josh asked. "I think Mitchell is planning to attend, and he could accompany Mom and Nancy."

"Yes, please." Jerilyn told him. "I'm so glad you called; I feel so much better. I'm going to Dad's tomorrow to get my mom's wedding gown, and plan to ask Austen's mother to make any alterations that are necessary. I love you."

"Love you, too."

~

Jerilyn called her dad and told him, "I want to come tomorrow to get Mom's dress. What time is good for you?"

"Any time, really. How about mid-morning?" he asked.

"Maybe we can have lunch together? My treat," she told him. "I'll pick you up, and you can pick the place."

"Sounds good to me. And you know I like Cinzetti's," he told her.

"Me too. I'll be by at eleven thirty."

~

After they had filled their plates and settled at their table, Jerilyn asked, "Why haven't we done this more often?" then reached for his hand and squeezed it. "I'm sorry, Dad."

"It's okay, kid. Let's don't voice any regrets, just enjoy today," he said. "How are things going with your wedding plans?"

"Okay," she told him. "I'm hoping I'll get the list from Josh and his mother today for invitations. It's late for sending them out. Maggie and Lainie are going to help me address them, and Jayden may help too. It's good one can get printing jobs done so quickly these days."

"Yes, I remember it was weeks for your mom and me from the time we ordered them 'til we picked them up. You mentioned that you weren't sure about attendants. Anything settled with that?" Jeff asked.

"Not really," Jerilyn told him, "but Josh suggested something that some might consider unusual. I probably do too, but the more I think about it, the more it seems like a good solution."

"Want to tell me about it?"

His daughter told him, "Not yet. Let's get back to the house and check out the gown."

~

Josh called to see if his mom was home. When she answered, he asked, "Do you have the list completed for the invitations?"

"I do," she told him. "Why don't you come for lunch, haven't really seen you since Jerilyn went back to Kansas."

"Sounds great. Don't have to be at TrailWays until later. Have an overnight trek that I'll be the wagon master for," he told her.

When his mother opened the door for him, he wrapped her in a hug and told her, "I love you, Mom."

"Where did that come from?" she asked. "I don't often hear that from you."

Josh told her, "I know, I'm sorry. Just want you to know I appreciate you and don't let you know like I should. Maybe it's Jerilyn's influence."

"You're missing her."

"Yeah, I know it's not that long before we're together, but it's still not soon enough."

"How are things progressing with the plans?" Mattie asked.

"Well, obviously, Jerilyn's got the main responsibilities for that. A couple of her friends are helping."

"Are you having attendants, and who?"

Josh told her, "That's not settled yet. But we have people in mind. I'll let you know later. I need the list now so I can get it to her. Think she wants to mail the invitations no later than tomorrow."

"I have it ready," his mother told him.

"Good. Now what's for lunch?"

~

The gown had been stored in a plastic case and hung in the closet in Jerilyn's folks' bedroom for thirty years. Her dad brought it out and laid it on the bed. She carefully unzipped it, and with the gown still on the hanger, held it up.

Memories came rushing back of the day her mother had showed it to her. Jerilyn could picture her smile as she talked about her wedding day. Joyce was as much in love with her husband, Jeff, as the day they married, and that had never changed.

Now Jerilyn wished she could feel her mother's arms around her as she did on that day. She thought of the country song she heard on the radio recently—Tim McGraw singing, "I Called Mama." How she wished she could call her mama.

And despite what her dad said earlier, there were regrets that she hadn't visited her mother more. And now she was going to be gone from here and parted from her dad. She vowed to herself that she would call him often.

Jeff watched the changing emotions wash across his daughter's face and went to her. He took the gown from her and placed it on the bed, then gathered her in his arms for a hug.

"Oh, Dad. I miss Josh so much and I want to be with him, but I'll miss you."

"I know," her dad said, "but it's not like we don't have ways of traveling to visit. Now, what do you think of the gown? Are you going to try it on now, or wait until you're at the Morgans'?"

Jerilyn put the gown back into the case and zipped it up. "I'll wait 'til I get there. Donna has made time for me today. I wonder if Linda will be there? I'd like to get better acquainted with her, even though I'm going to be gone. After all," she said with a smile in her voice, "she may be a sister-in-law someday. And your daughter-in-law."

As it turned out, there was little to do to the gown. Its fit was almost as if it had been made for Jerilyn. After the few alterations and a special cleaning, it would be perfect for that special day.

Donna told her, "Your mom would be so happy seeing you in her gown. I'm glad you and Josh were able to finally work out all the difficulties in your relationship. I guess overall, it took longer than it took Austen and Mark, and that was long enough."

"I can imagine how hard those days and weeks and months were for them," Jerilyn said. "I almost couldn't function those months when Josh and I weren't communicating. Though maybe it wasn't quite so bad for them, since they at least were together and knew what was happening with the other. All kinds of scenarios were marching through my mind. But I would tell myself, we don't really know each other anyway; I'm probably expecting too much."

Donna let Jerilyn finish her thoughts, then told her, "I should be able to make those few changes in a couple of days. I'll let you know."

While she was still dressed in the gown, Linda walked in.

"Oh, you're beautiful! Hi, Jerilyn."

"And hello to you, Linda. Where are you flying these days? Any exotic places?"

"No," she told her. "Lately, I've just been flying in the States, no international flights for some time. That means I get to be home more."

Donna spoke up and said, "Not that she's actually here that much." Then to Jerilyn, "Do you need help getting out of the dress?"

"If you'll unzip it, I think I can manage," she told her.

Jerilyn saw the blush on Linda's face at her mother's words, but chose not to say anything.

Then Linda said, "Well, I guess I do spend a lot of time with Jon. Though his work shifts limit that too." Then turning to Jerilyn as she left the room, she asked, "Will you have time to visit for a while?"

"I was hoping you would be here, so we can," Jerilyn told her. "I'll yell if I need help."

As she entered the room where Linda was waiting, Jerilyn told her, "I've been thinking how much time I spent with Austen, but I hardly know you."

"Well, she did have David and her job, and I was flying around the world," Linda responded. "Plus, I'm young enough to not be involved with her group of friends. I know you all have been a great support for her. And now, she's so happy it almost hurts to be around her."

"I know what you mean," Jerilyn agreed. "I'm praying the love Josh and I have will be as strong."

"I do too," Linda told her. "That's the way marriages should be. You know Jon and I have been dating." Jerilyn nodded, then Linda continued, "We're taking it slow, as some might say. Guess we feel the same way; we want to be sure that our love is real and forever."

"Be glad you have that option," Jerilyn told her. "Your sister fell in love with a man who was determined not to love. And I fell in love with a man who lives miles away. It would have been so much better, and not so heartbreaking, if the beginning had been different. And not that it matters, but I think you're perfect for my brother. Maybe you both can come visit us in Nebraska some time."

"We will, have already discussed it. And it does matter to me what you think," Linda told her.

Donna joined them, and the three visited a bit longer before Jerilyn said, "This has been great. But I need to get home and start addressing invitations. Some people are going to wonder why they didn't get them sooner."

Twenty Six

With the help of Jerilyn's friends, most of the preparations for the wedding were completed, and replies to the invitations came every day. There would be a good crowd.

She and Josh hardly missed a day calling each other, with texts and emails in between. He still hadn't told her his idea for the honeymoon. He wanted it to be secret and hoped it would please her.

With only a few days before he came to Overland Park, and not many more before the wedding, they finally addressed the question of the attendants.

He reminded her, "We talked, however briefly, about asking our parents. What are you thinking now?"

Jerilyn told him, "As I first said, it's not a usual occurrence, but considering everything, I believe it will be a sweet element."

"But what if they say 'no', and we can't convince them otherwise? It's late to ask anyone else. And do you plan to wear a tuxedo? I hadn't even thought about that."

"Do you remember the suit Mark wore at his wedding?" Josh asked.

"Yes, with its neat western cut. I liked that suit."

"I have one very similar," Josh told her, "and I hoped it would work."

"And do you plan to wear boots too?"

"Well, yes. They're about the only kind of shoes I have. Unless you don't want me to?"

"The suit probably wouldn't look right with plain old shoes," Jerilyn said with a smile. "And I'm sure Dad has a suit that will be appropriate, or it could even be a good excuse to get a new one."

"Getting back to the attendant's question, we won't know what our parents will say until we ask," Josh said. "So the next question is, who will do the asking? Do I ask my mom and you ask your dad? Or the other way around?"

"How about you ask Dad? You can tell him about your suit and talk about what he might wear. So that leaves me to call your mother. What do you think?"

"Sounds good to me. When?"

"Let's do it tomorrow." Without giving him a chance to answer, she asked, "Where are we going on our honeymoon?"

"Yes to tomorrow. No to the honeymoon."

"I've never been good with surprises," she said.

"Trust me," Josh told her. "I love you. I won't do anything to cause you angst."

~

Jerilyn started to call Mattie first thing, then remembered it was an hour earlier in Plattsford, giving her a bit more time to consider what she would say. "Hi, Mattie. How are you doing? Want to be my matron of honor?" Probably not.

Knowing it would be at least an hour before she would make the call, she returned to her room and opened the closet doors. It was time to start packing for her move to Nebraska.

~

Josh's alarm woke him, and he reached to turn it off. First thing on his mind was Jerilyn, as it was every morning. Not that many days before she would be his. What a journey it had been. He remembered that day he met her at TrailWays, when he greeted her in his usual flirtatious way, no idea how important she would become to him. Then came that lost desert of time after Mark and Austen's wedding. He realized by then that he loved her, though there had been no kiss.

There was no declaration to each other, nor had they shared their feelings with their friends. Which led to those friends misinterpreting incidents they noticed involving the two, which were then voiced to the other in texts and emails. It was months before the misinformation was corrected.

Now, this day, today, he would call her dad to ask if he would serve as his best man for their wedding.

~

"Hello," Jeff answered.

"Hi, it's Josh."

"I see that. What can I help you with?"

"It has to do with the wedding," Josh told him. "Jerilyn and I have discussed who to have for our attendants."

"Oh, did you want to talk to Jon?"

"Well, no," Josh said. We thought that if you two agreed, we would have our parents. And yes, we know that most people might consider that unusual."

"So, I'm asking you, will you serve as my best man?"

Taken aback, Jeff was silent, then said, "I would be honored. Will I need a tuxedo?"

Josh told him, "That will be up to you, but I'm wearing a western-cut suit that I already have. A regular Sunday suit would be fine."

"We don't usually dress up for church these days," Jeff told him. "But I do have a suit that would probably fit right in. Not really western cut, but close enough. It's black; will that be okay?"

~

Mattie answered the phone, "Good morning."

"And to you," Jerilyn responded.

"As 'they' say," Mattie said, "to what do I owe this pleasure?"

"I have a request and hope you won't find it too unusual," Jerilyn told her.

"Oh, you have whetted my curiosity. Ask away."

After a short pause, Jerilyn asked, "Will you be my matron of honor?"

There was no answer for a while. "But what about your friends?"

"You can probably guess that if it was a different time of year, we would have asked Mark and Austen," Jerilyn told her. "Now, besides the responsibilities of TrailWays, there's her pregnancy."

Mattie asked, "Does Josh have a best man?" thinking it would be awkward if he was a young man.

"My dad."

At first, Mattie wasn't sure she had heard correctly, then, "Your dad?"

Then, "Yes."

"You said yes?" Jerilyn asked.

"Yes," with a laugh. "Now I need to know how to dress, what length it should be. And what about the color?"

Jerilyn told her, "Whatever you feel comfortable with. I'll be wearing my mom's wedding gown. Josh will be in his western-cut suit. I think he said it's black. And my dad's suit is black—not a tuxedo."

"What about your bouquet?" Mattie asked. "Any special color?"

"It's going to be wildflowers—sunflowers for sure, and whatever else the florist can come up with. Maybe gay feather, larkspur, coneflower, Culver's root. She showed a picture of one to me. It was beautiful," Jerilyn told her.

"I believe I have the perfect dress," Mattie said. "It's pale blue with a lace overlay, waltz length. It can fill the function of groom's mother's dress as well as matron of honor. I can email a picture if you like."

"If you want to, though it's not necessary, sounds beautiful."

~

With the question about attendants settled, there was little left to do before the wedding, just a week away. The days had seemed to drag, busy as they were, since Jerilyn had last been with Josh. She was glad they decided he would come early, and this was the day.

Her dad and brothers all offered to make the trip to the airport. But she wanted to go herself, not wanting to wait longer than necessary to touch him again, to hug him again, to kiss him again. And Josh was feeling the same way, hoping it would be Jerilyn who met him at the end of this hopefully last journey without her.

He was standing at the curb with his luggage when she drove up, parked her car and ran to where he stood with his arms open. As others walked past, there was the touch, the hug, and kiss which they had both yearned for. But they were interrupted when a security car parked behind Jerilyn's. Quickly loading Josh's luggage, they waved at the smiling guard as they pulled away.

When they were on I-29, heading for I-635 and toward Overland Park, Jerilyn asked, "Did you remember the rings?"

"Yes, I did, and everything else I need for a couple of weeks."

She gave him a quick look at that, and asked, "Two weeks? It's just a week until the wedding. Do you think it will take a week to pack and drive to Plattsford?"

"I hope not," Josh answered.

"Then what?"

"Our honeymoon." At another startled look from Jerilyn, he said, "Yes, I remember you don't like surprises. But I hope this will be a good one. You told me once about a cruise you wouldn't mind taking. I did ask Austen and your brothers and dad about it. So, what about Cozumel?"

"Oh my! If I wasn't driving, I would hug you."

"Only a hug? I'd like more than that."

~

He was staying with Jeff and Jon the week before the wedding, so Jerilyn drove directly there. He got out of the car and went around to assist her.

"Now you can give me that hug, and maybe a kiss?"

Jeff came out of the house and asked if he could help with the luggage.

"Sure can," Josh told him. "Jerilyn is just thanking me for her surprise."

Noticing Jeff's raised eyebrows and questioning look, he explained, "The honeymoon."

"Ah," Jeff nodded and took the bag holding Josh's suit.

Jerilyn said to her dad, "I can't believe you all were able to keep it secret."

When Josh's belongings were unloaded and settled in the room he would be using, they went to the kitchen where Jeff had coffee. After a few minutes of catching up, Josh and Jerilyn left to drive to her house.

~

When Jerilyn pulled into her driveway, another car followed. She checked her rearview mirror to see who it might be. Jack's patrol car was there, meaning he was inside, so it wasn't him. When she got out of her car, the other driver did the same, and she saw that it was Derek. She heard a snicker from the house and turned to see Jack standing in the doorway.

Without noticing Josh, who was standing at the car door, Derek came up to Jerilyn and said, "There you are; haven't seen you lately, and your brother doesn't tell me anything. What's going on in your life? Are you getting ready for school?"

Josh couldn't wait any longer and walked past Derek to Jerilyn, put his arm around her, and said, "She's been getting engaged to me and we're getting married next week. Anything else you want to know?"

Derek looked from one to the other, then without saying anything, returned to his car, backed out of the driveway, and proceeded down the street.

Jack came to shake Josh's hand and hug his sister, and, still laughing, said, "I'm so glad I saw that."

Jerilyn asked, "Did you have something to do with his being here?"

Jack admitted, "Well, maybe. Jayden and I saw him at Cinzetti's. He asked about you, and I told him you had to make a trip to the airport but should be here this afternoon. I really didn't think he would come by; thought he would call or text."

"You're still my mischievous little brother. He has left a few messages. I've just ignored them."

Josh asked, "What's his name?"

"Derek." Jack looked toward his sister. "Does he have a last name?"

"Ireland," she told him.

"Maybe we can introduce him to Anita," Josh said. "They could be another Kansas-Nebraska couple. And appropriate: Ireland, O'Neill, almost serendipitous."

"Sure, that's going to happen," Jerilyn said.

"Well you never know," Josh told her. "From what he said, he must be a teacher, and so is she. They could meet at a conference."

"Enough about those two; let's go inside," Jerilyn said.

Even while Jerilyn was working on wedding plans, she and Jack had pursued the possibility of his buying her house, and perhaps most of the furniture. By the time Josh arrived, those plans were almost complete. There were some special things she would like to keep and move to Nebraska, wondering how they would fit in Josh's fully furnished home. With that in mind, she wanted to walk through her house with him and point them out.

Josh told her, "If you want them, there is no question. You can take anything you want. We can figure out the best place for them when we get there."

Time moved on, as it had a way of doing. The things to be moved to Nebraska were gathered in one place, and clothes packed for the honeymoon. Jerilyn's brothers arranged for a limo to pick up the couple at the house for their trip to the airport.

Josh's mother and sister and Mitchell arrived late afternoon the day before the rehearsal. Mattie and Nancy were staying at a hotel, and Mitchell with his cousin.

Jeff and Mattie's first meeting was at the rehearsal, but it took little time for them to become acquainted. Those who didn't know them would have thought they were long-time friends.

Neither they, nor Jerilyn and Josh, had told the others that their parents were to be the attendants. Thus, all the young people: Nancy and Mitchell, Jack and Jayden, and Jon and Linda, were curious and looking at each other, wondering. Maybe they weren't having attendants? The only others present for the rehearsal were the pastor and his wife, who weren't sure either, expecting it could be all of the young people who were there.

Pastor Bradley said, "Well, let's get started. Will the bride and groom and any attendants come forward? We'll go over a few things, then practice the ceremony."

When Mattie and Jeff stood to join Jerilyn and Josh, there was applause and smiles. Reaction to this atypical choice of attendants was all positive, with the young couples looking forward to seeing what the response would be from the wedding guests the next day.

Ladies from church had prepared a meal for them, so after practicing the walk up the aisle and the ceremony a couple of times, all of them moved to the room where it was being served. The small venue made it easy to visit and get acquainted. Jerilyn was grateful for this special time with her father and brothers. There was lively conversation about the distance from Overland Park to Plattsford, and mention of possible future visits.

This was the first time she had seen her brothers interact with Jayden and Linda. And as she watched all the couples, Jerilyn wondered if it might be a look into the future. If that should turn out to be so, at least there wouldn't be a time of separation for any of them.

She reached for Josh's hand and whispered to him, "I'm thanking God that our times of being apart are over."

He raised her hand to his lips. "Me too. And I'm thanking Him for you."

~

It was a perfect day for the wedding. Sunny, but cool for August. The church was filled with friends and family. Most of those from Overland Park had not met Josh, but knew he must be a special person if Jerilyn had chosen him.

There was music from Ron's Band and a video her brothers had put together depicting their lives and times together. Mark and Austen sent some CDs so Josh could be included.

Then the video cut off and the music changed. The back doors opened, and Josh entered with his mother. Whispers could be heard among the guests as he escorted her to her position in the front, hugged her, then moved to his place.

At that, the band started playing "Here Comes the Bride." Everyone stood and turned to face the back. It was time. Jerilyn entered on her father's arm. When they reached the front, Jeff kissed her, then placed her hand in Josh's. When it was time for the vows, she passed her bouquet to Mattie. The couple had already said all their special words to each other, so the vows were traditional.

Then the rings, and they were a married couple.

And, "You may kiss the bride."

Their first kiss of this unforgettable day, and their first as a married couple.

~

Ron's Band had moved on and set up for the reception, playing the popular songs of the day, as well as R & B, and Motown. The band was highly requested for weddings, but Ron had made a special effort to be available for this one.

Then, the first dance. With his arms around his bride, Josh told Jerilyn, "After all our travels, this is the sweetest journey—the beginning of our life together. No more separations, no more need to travel. How hard it was, but how glad I am that it happened, so I can be with you, and now it's forever."

About the Author

Anne Edmondson Barbour grew up on a farm, the only girl in the family, with three brothers. She has always liked to read and write, and read every book in the library for her age before she was six years old. She has also penned articles for newsletters and genealogical publications.

Anne is now retired, a genealogist and lover of history, and a true romantic. She can envision romance in any circumstance or background, leading to her desire to author novels. She and her late husband married two months and two days after their first date.

After retiring, the couple presented many historic reenactment programs, including the Oregon Trail migration. Dressed in period clothing, they became well known for their endeavors, and received many accolades and requests for presentations.

Now widowed, Anne has five children; ten grandchildren; four step-grandchildren; six great-grandchildren; and one step-great-grandchild scattered throughout the country and overseas.

Made in the USA
Monee, IL
28 February 2021

61154225R00144